KAIJU CATACLYSM

SAM M. PHILLIPS

KAIJU CATACLYSM

WWW.SEVEREDPRESS.COM

ISBN: 978-1-923165-41-0

1

I am Godrisaur.

With my deafening roar and monstrous might, you may think I am alien to you, that my thoughts are so different from yours. But see in my wild temper and violent glory the sameness of our being, for we are born of the same soil, the same Earth. I am not an alien from another world; I am a force of nature.

Look inside your own savage mind and see my reflection there, a cold pool, staring back, with ripples shaking the surface, spreading to the edges in wicked, jagged circles. Each of them is like a ring in the cut-down world-tree, marking the years until the final doom comes to pass, when one such as I manifests to this plane, ready to reap you.

I do not come to harvest humans—not as humans see themselves, the body—I come for souls. I come from the deep for the deep.

I come to kill Gods.

I am reborn, returned to the world to kill you.

To kill you all.

***

Marc woke with a start, his skin itching him like crazy. He'd been having the same dream again, the same horrific nightmare. He got up, scratching at his arms and legs, and made himself a drink. No alcohol, but a tablet dropped in water, fizzing away, quickly turning the yellow of urine, which he quaffed with the relish of a drowning man gulping air. The fizz burnt his throat, but calmed his nerves enough for his skin to not feel like fire. Still he scratched, as if trying to unconsciously rid himself of the psychological burden of his dream. It replayed like an old movie, seen many times, now memorized, flashing across the inside of his eyelids every time he blinked.

"Damn it all to hell," he gasped, going back to bed, loathe to turn the light on, though desperately wanting to write something. The blank, unwritten pages taunted him in the dark, the empty notebooks there on the nightstand. "It never seems like I can do enough."

He was referring to all the books he wanted to write so badly but couldn't concentrate enough to finish. There were ideas inside him which wanted to spring forth into life, but his scattered mind ran wild before their furious assault, as if fleeing, frightened by some primordial beast he witnessed there in the subconscious caves of his soul.

"Must you destroy everything?" he said to himself quietly, not wanting to wake his girlfriend, Jain. She fussed in her sleep beside him.

"Must you take all the blankets?" she said sleepily, not opening her eyes. He growled, annoyed at this reprimand from her when he was doing his best for her, lying silently in the dark so as not to disturb her.

"Don't you think I want to be comfortable, too?" he said, or thought, readjusting the hot water bottle in the bed, which was still quite hot; definitely a bad sign.

It mustn't be that far through the night, he thought. *And here I am, fretting like a freak. Tomorrow, or today, I suppose, I have to get up and work, and I'll be as tired as yesterday, or today, and nothing much will get done again.*

In the dark he turned to the books beside the bed. He considered turning the light on, reading at least a few of the pages, but instead a monster beckoned him, drawing him back into the pit of his mind. His thoughts were visceral and visual.

I can see gore and sprayed blood. I can see toppled cities. I can see something, lurking there in the dark depths of the world, living in an ocean deeper than humanity ever thought possible.

***

He awoke again, this time even more panicked for he hadn't realized he'd fallen asleep again. Or was this the first time?

He saw a number flash across his mind—three sixes—and he was sitting at a desk. The light was on. He wasn't in his bedroom with his sleeping girlfriend. Instead, he'd been working.

When had that happened?

The number had progressed beyond six six six before his eyes, now reading seven something something, growing all the time. Other little numbers, and many, many letters danced along his vision like bouncing balls.

I see heads rolling. They are the heads of dismembered people...

Shocked, he blinked, and wondered how he'd gotten here. He looked around the room, tried to take in the space. It was an office. There were many boxes. In them were tiny monsters, miniature model kits waiting to be assembled and painted. Next to his dancing hands were small pots of paints. He considered cracking one open and drinking it, though with the names on them—things like 'Abyssal Black' and 'Agitated Pink'—they sounded toxic. Memories of what they tasted like came to him, but only in tiny little snippets, as if a hummingbird was darting its tongue into his mouth, feeding him poisonous chemical nectar in minute portions.

"Fuck, but my feet are cold," he said.

But my fingers run hot.

They were moving. He was typing.

"Holy shit, am I actually writing?"

***

I am being created. I am created by you. But you are not the one who writes words. You are the one who hears words.

I speak. I am both a God and the killer of Gods. I am the dark reflection of the bright one who made the physical universe. I am the second verse, a whispered shadow.

Do you really believe that the reptile part of your brain is so stupid it could not be cognizant? Here I am, pulsing at the back of your head.

Drip, drip come the thoughts. Tip tap flows the oozing blood, pulsing through that part of you.

The dread beast is not outside. The phone call is not coming from inside the house. It is coming from inside your mind.

I will speak to you there. I will become you there.

And then you will die, because I am hungry, and I must feed. One of us must be destroyed, and it won't be me. You can die and I live on, because while you conjure me with these thoughts, I multiply, becoming alive in the mind of the next one to read these words. I am back there, in the base of their brains also. I infect them with fear and run through their blood. Their skin quakes as yours does. I am a parasite, mounting you and sucking you dry.

I am Godrisaur.

I speak.

***

"Holy shit," Marc repeated. "Did I write that?"

He looked at the page. It flashed a million times a second, refreshing itself, a mirror of his own senses, of the intake of light hitting his eyes, transmitted to his brain.

"Who wrote that?"

He looked over his shoulder, feeling a presence there.

***

I am not back there.

I am back here.

I am in the brain stem. I am the reptile. Feel me pulse. I am the heartbeat. I am the doorway. I am the shadow shapes, hiding from you until it is too late.

But I am not hiding anymore. I am revealing myself.

So, yes, it is too late.

Too late for you, Marc.

2

"Geez, it must be late," Marc said, looking at the clock in the bottom right of his screen. It was 1:00am, still early by the standards of someone somewhere. He glanced at the bottom left of his screen, saw that he'd reached nearly double the word count from the last time he'd watched that number rise.

"Do you really think any of this is worth anything?" he said, pondering what he had made, if those numbers actually meant he could be at peace.

But no, my skin still crawls.

This time it was his belly; he felt a gnawing there. It wasn't his own hunger but the hunger of something else, something that was eating *him.*

It was coming from within.

"Is it a parasite, something small and insidious?"

His brain beat like a heart.

Thump, thump, thump.

It was a heavy lump, pumping up and down, flexing in and out. It felt as if the organ was too big for his skull, seeking to burst free from its confines, continuing to expand until it was huge and all-encompassing, enough to enshroud the whole planet with his dark thoughts.

"Or is it a monster, huge and menacing, able to raze cities to the ground?"

***

You think I can be contained with such human concepts of size? Of course, I am both large and small. My body is within your body, small as a thought, as imperceptible as the turning of the micro-machinery within each of your cells. Yet I have a body which is external to you, which can rip you apart and feast upon your flesh and drink your blood.

I am in the ocean now, bubbling like a dormant volcano. Look! Turn your head and see me contained in one of those boxes on your shelf. I am a plastic toy, a product of someone's imagination, carved into pieces to be more easily stored away. But when I am put back together, like some type of Frankenstein's monster, I will be living and potent again.

You can drink those paints all you like, because all it will do is help color me further. And when every little piece of me is black, orange, and burning red, I will come forth, ripping apart the plastic wrapping, tearing open the printed cardboard, and I will be everything to you, much more than some base creation of the mind. I will be a beating heart you choke on, filling up your mouth with blood, suffocating you so that I may feed, live.

***

"Don't drink the paint," Marc told himself, eying up the paint pot with the delicious and enticing label 'Crimson Gore.'

"Don't drink the paint."

***

I am all Gods because I eat the flesh of Gods. I am a hunter, a master.

I make the ocean boil. I make the blood within your veins pop like candy. You are the water I drink, the liquid I become. I am like the sun, with its burning tendrils, reaching for you in the day. Yes, even in the day I hunt you, the sun no longer a source of pleasure but a device of torture, screaming at you silently. The waking hours are not a sanctuary, a time when the shadows retreat and all seems like a bad dream.

There is nowhere I can't find you, nowhere that is safe.

***

"I must be mad," Marc said. He'd caught himself wishing for it to be daytime already, for the dark of night to be banished. But the night was the only thing soothing his open wounds, the cool liquid air flowing up through his siphon toes to reach into the inner spaces of his body, where molten lava flowed like the writhing flesh of a monster.

"I can see it coming to life," he said, referring to that monster. "It has magma scales and bloody eyes. With its mouth it bites upon a sun, the light chomping into pieces as it works its massive jaws."

***

You see the power to destroy worlds. You see the radioactive heart of a planet, a gift of the Gods bestowed upon me. I am the keeper of the key. I am the one with the bomb. When I speak, cities burn; with my words bones turn to ash.

***

So, I didn't just think this thing up? This monster is real? Marc asked himself silently. *It exists somewhere outside of me?*

"In the depths of the oceans, yes," he said, not realizing he was going to speak. He felt the words come forth with the burn of a hot curry. They had an acid tang to them, as if there were chemicals behind them. It was his own bile, and he choked on it.

Then his stomach rumbled. He realized he was going to puke as its contents flipped and landed again like a rabbit punch.

He rushed to the toilet.

***

I open my mouth and release the power—a ray of sunshine, a laser beam, a cannon roaring. It boils the ocean. It kills fish in the millions. They do not float to the surface, with the mystery of their death to be puzzled over by passing fishermen. They are atomized, turned to vapor alongside the water, which rises into the sky, marring the atmosphere with a stain seen on the scientific devices of man.

***

"What the hell is that?" said Marc, returning to his computer, wiping the last of the vomit from his mouth with the sleeve of his jumper. It was a weather warning on the bottom bar of his computer screen, flashing red next to some words that didn't make sense to him. He took the mouse, hovered it over the angry looking icon.

Words popped up in a grey box: 'Low pressure system, high winds, spike in temperature, a potential cyclone forming in the center of the Pacific Ocean.'

Marc frowned, not sure if he'd read that right. Did it even make scientific sense? He was no meteorologist, so he didn't have the expertise to challenge it if it didn't. There was a graphic representation trying to make the whole thing simpler, but it was all nonsense to him, turning like a kaleidoscope into new shapes, new colors each second.

***

I am reborn. I rotate in a circle, gradually increasing in speed and tempo. I whip the elements into a frenzy. I make storms. I *am* storms. I am a force of nature.

***

The winds swirled around a central point.

"Is this some type of live feed?" asked Marc, absentmindedly turning a box on his shelf with his hand. A gigantic bird wreathed in lightning was displayed on its cover and he inspected it closely. "Geez, imagine if it was real?" he said, not sure if he meant the giant elemental avian or the bizarre weather system. He put the box down and went back to his desk and sat down. The seat gave him a jolt of static electricity, making him jump. He looked at it accusingly, his glare a silent warning for it not to repeat such a cruel prank.

With tentative movements, as if lowering himself into a scalding hot bath, he sat back down. He sighed with relief that there was no shock, nor any burning pain of boiling water. There was just…nothing; the absence of pain as good as the presence of pleasure.

***

Find no comfort in the temporary relief of the senses, because they cannot keep you from death. They will not allow you to hide from me. Children run for their beds, get under the covers, placing a thin veil of warmth and softness between them and me. It is nothing but a psychological balm. It soothes but does not protect. You are merely ignorant of that which you fear. It is forgetfulness, nothing more.

The source of your terror is still out there.

I am still out there.

***

Marc's eyes jiggled in their sockets, tracing a circle around the edges of the computer screen, not wanting to look directly at the information it displayed.

It wasn't the weather report he was avoiding. It was his own words, the ones he'd been typing without thinking.

"I don't want to know what they say," he said to himself, knowing they revealed a horrifying truth he didn't want to confront. Couldn't confront.

A cyclone was forming. It was either inside him, in his mind, his soul…or outside, in the world, in the ocean.

Or it was both.

***

I *am* real. If anything is conjured by the mind, then it is real. Thoughts are the birth of all things, even a monster such as me.

***

Marc got up, needing to ground himself back in reality. He made coffee, went to the toilet to piss.

Everything which goes in must come out, he thought, and the faux-profundity of that made him laugh.

"If that's the case, what do I allow in which makes me produce such things," he said, referring to the monster he knew was lurking in the other room.

But it wasn't in the other room; it was in his head, following him, watching.

***

Yes, I watch. I see you.

***

Marc turned, expecting to find someone standing there behind him. Instead there was just the back door of his house, the one leading out through the laundry. It rattled with a gust of wind.

Has that wind come off the Pacific Ocean? Has it been carried here all the way from the site of whatever created that strange weather system?

Another gust of wind made him jump in fright, and he fled into the living room. He heard a monster growl there, as if it was looking out at him from its dark cave, sensing a morsel to be devoured. His stomach swirled sickeningly and he tasted vomit again, the burning bile in his throat making his back teeth ache. Grimacing, he scanned the room, heard rather than saw the air conditioning unit was on. He looked at it out of the corner of his eye, as if trying to catch it in the act before it could switch off again.

Did I turn that on?

Hot air pumped from it, the stinking hot breath of the beast. Steam rose from coffee on the table beside his hand. Both fogged up his glasses.

I don't wear glasses.

He rubbed his eyes, which made strange grinding sounds, as if there was grit deeply ingrained.

Oh, God, I'm so tired. I'm fried.

***

In my anger and frustration, I unleash another vomiting stream of power. It burns through a whale, killing a species of this creature larger and rarer than any of the tiny specimens mankind has detected so much closer to the surface.

I am in a deep fissure. I am in a trench at the bottom of the ocean. It is normally dark here, but I illuminate the stygian blackness with my energy. I glow hot. I burn the water, killing the impossibly big creatures, the Gods of their domain no more.

The vaporized ocean swirls above me, opening a portal to the sky, to the world of the surface. It is my birth canal. I look up through it, see the second sun, the one that did not create me, and I smile, my teeth as big as the ships of man.

Though I am newly made, I remember such things, such shapes, such creations, because I have lived before. In ancient times, and in the future, I have existed in the oceans, and on the land. I am the dinosaurs of the past and the forthcoming mutant reptiles. I straddle time like the God I am. I *am* time.

I am dimensions themselves. I eat them. I shit them out.

***

"Fuck, that coffee's hit quick," said Marc, not referring to the fact he felt more awake, but rather that he suddenly felt a stirring deep in his bowels. "Why does it always do this to me?"

He ran to the toilet, sat down, and slid a smooth poo out. It dropped into the water like a depth charge, splashing his anus with wet coldness. He laughed at the tickling sensation.

"If only novels fell from me so easily," he said, wiping his butt. He glanced into the toilet at the messy pile of shit. "And were so beautiful."

He saw Rorschach patterns there. It was a face, or two faces, two lovers kissing. It both repelled and attracted him. He leaned forward, but then the foul vapors rising from the crap hit him. In reflex, he quickly struck the flush button. The shit swirled, taking the corrupt miasma with it, down into the depths, and all of it was sucked away.

But not really, it never really leaves. The shit just goes somewhere else, rises in some other, bigger bog.

Out in the middle of the Pacific Ocean, in the toilet of the world, a monster stirred, rising from the deep.

***

I go up, up, up, climbing through steam and bubbles. Or, at least, that is my fantasy. In reality, I rise through gore and blood, the boiled skeletons of fish falling past me like cascading rain. I live on the back of Death. I am an avatar of Death. I am the waste of the world, coalesced into a bright ball of vengeance. Is the Earth sick of the tiny men on the surface? It wants to shake them off like the fleas they are. I am hungry for fleas. If they carry pestilence, then I am a plague eater. I regurgitate the Black Death upon them like the ocean regurgitates me. It spits me out, a lump of black bile.

I am a cancer.

I come to kill the body from the inside.

***

Marc could feel the mounting dread itching on the back of his eyeballs. It was like a rat was back there, scratching his eyes because it couldn't scratch away the fleas which tormented it.

Why does it want to come out through my eyes?

He thought about a torture method he'd read about. Placing a rat on a person's stomach, they covered it with an overturned bowl. When hot coals were piled on top of the bowl, the rat, in a frenzy to escape the heat, ate through the unfortunate human's skin, gnawed through their guts.

The rat was inside the person. It entered them, became part of them, only emerging when they'd been hollowed out...or else became them.

Do we become someone if we eat them?

***

I consume flesh. The whales and giant squids—monsters one and all—are but morsels to me, tidbits to sate my hunger for a moment. Devouring them barely achieves this, and I am ravenous for more. I want to eat a whole race. I feel the pulse of mankind on the surface.

I see through to another place, watching from the back of a pair of eyes, and there, in the reflection of a mirror, I see the single entity. They are the representative of everything I will become when their flesh fills my mouth.

***

Marc looked in the mirror. Dark hair framed a face reminiscent of a handsome rat, scars hidden by ragged stubble, the skin hanging loose with bone weariness. He leaned in, not able to tell if his eyeballs were jiggling, perhaps *because* they were jiggling, meaning he couldn't focus on them. Or were they vibrating at the same speed as he was seeing them vibrate, thus canceling each other out?

"There's no rats back there, man, you're just up way too late and you've drunk too much coffee. Now you're seeing shit, and feeling shit, and making stuff up," he said.

Isn't that what writers are meant to do?

He went back to the keyboard and wrote that down. Then he deleted it and tried to write something better. But there was nothing better so he wrote it again. Or, at least, he typed it out, which was what most writers do most of the time. If they thought at all it was very shallowly, and Marc more shallowly than most.

It wasn't that he was dumb, or that he didn't think. He tried to get out of his own way, not interpose his conscious interpretations upon the work. He wanted to pull what was deep and subconscious up to the surface, even if it was ugly, and examine it in the light.

The only problem was that once it was unleashed it could do real damage.

3

Marc heard someone shuffling down the hall like a zombie. They turned the corner, peered in, face pale in the half light of the room, the only illumination coming from the computer screen.

"What are you doing?" asked Jain, squinting into the gloom and rubbing her eyes. She'd had her hair dyed and treated the previous day, and it cascaded around her face in blonde waves in a way which made Marc's heart sing.

"I'm writing, I'm okay," he said.

"I was worried. I could hear something, like bones cracking."

"Just me typing. I started a new book. It's called—"

"You sure you're okay? Because when you get up in the night, sometimes you get a bit…weird."

"I'm weird but okay. The weird is going into the book!" he said, louder than he had intended.

"Bring the energy down a bit, I'm half asleep."

"I woke up itchy for some reason and couldn't stand lying in the dark any longer, so I decided to get up. Look, I've written so much already."

She didn't look, or answer, but instead turned and shuffled back down the hall, a zombie once more. He got up and went after her.

"I promise I'm alright. It's cold, isn't it?" he said.

"Yes, I want to go back to bed."

"I love you so much," he cooed, hugging her. "I'm going to love you forever."

She hugged him back. He knew what he said had some special gravity today, as yesterday had been his parents' fifty-fourth wedding anniversary. The family had gone out to dinner. The relaxing atmosphere of the event had been a reminder of the good things in life, and of the pleasure of love and commitment.

"Maybe I ate a bit too much at dinner," he said. "And that's why I'm up. Don't know why I'm itchy though." He rubbed his eyeballs, could feel the rat scratching back there again. Actually, he could hear it.

"Oh, that rat is back," she said. This scared him.

"You can hear it?" he asked, incredulous.

"Yes," she said and went to pee. The hissing of her piss momentarily overcame the sound of scratching. When she was done, and finished rustling the covers of the bed as she climbed into it, he listened intently. The scratching was definitely there, but it wasn't coming from his head.

It was coming from the walls.

***

The walls of the world rise up to defy me like the battlements of a castle. I smash them down, for I am mighty and filled with primordial power. These mountains of water, rising and falling, are nothing, and the ocean's gargantuan waves break against me as if against a stout lighthouse. Like the lighthouse, my foundation goes right down to the bedrock. I stand on an underwater ridge. I stride along this promontory, making my way for the coast, very far away. But to me the distance isn't so great, my legs long, my pace inexorable. I will make it to land. I will make it to the human cities. Though I am a creature of the sea, born in water, it is actually with rock I have my deepest connection, with the fabric of the Earth itself. I am made of cooled magma, built from the hot, liquid heart of the world.

With my feet upon the solid, dry ground, I will be unstoppable. None shall stand in my way.

***

Marc stared at the page. Something had stopped him writing. The cursor blinked mockingly, challenging him to continue. He took a deep breath, willing himself to overcome this invisible obstacle. He knew the barrier was nothing but himself, but that it had power nonetheless. It could conjure up false narratives, and more besides, to prevent him from having the will to continue. He looked down at his fingers. They felt hard and stiff, like stone. He picked them up and dropped them onto the keyboard, plunging once more into the icy waters of his soul.

***

I gaze down at the puny things floating on the water. They may be bigger than the mighty whales, longer than the trailing tentacles of the sea squid, but they are still small. And where those dignified creatures were proud flesh, these are abominable metal. For all their jagged hardness and too-perfect lines, however, they are still fragile.

Battleships, war-machines, floating coffins—these are the creations of creatures with no natural defenses beyond their own mad imaginations. With weapons they project this fake might, exposing their own frailty and fear.

The human ships blossom with fiery explosions spouted from barrels pointing like judgmental fingers, the accusation plain: I am not like them and must be destroyed.

I feel the tiny stings of impacts on my molten scales. It is not pain, though, only a tapping at the door. They do not gain entrance and I will not admit them. If this is all they can muster to stop me, then it is as nothing.

I smash down with my fist. I do not bother to strike the battleships themselves, but rather the water nearby. The shock to the surface is so sudden and mighty it is as if I have struck a pane of glass rather than a liquid. The surface shatters and breaks apart, my fist punching through. Then a giant pluming spout of water rushes up through the hole I've made. It lifts into the sky, expanding like the mushroom cloud of an atomic bomb. White and blue crystals sparkle malevolently, as if filled with malignant radioactivity. They rain down like exploded fragments of a ruptured diamond, landing in a heavy sheet, churning the ocean's surface to furious froth. This impact forms waves that cascade one into the other, building until they are a tsunami. The humungous waves smash the ships aside like the dismissive hand of a contemptuous God.

I am that God. And I stride on through the broken flotsam and jetsam mingling on the surface of the turbulent sea.

***

Marc was in turmoil, struggling to find the will to continue. It had been hours. The bottom right of the screen read a different number than before, so did the one in the bottom left; both denoted progress, but also fatigue. It was so late. The book was getting old, and tired, the writing stale.

Stale. He got up and pulled the bread out of the bag. It felt hard.

"Perhaps it'll be better toasted," he said and popped the pieces in the toaster. "Everything is better with a little heat applied."

He leaned over the toaster, watched the coils burn bright orange. He saw in them the skin of the monster, the way it fed on energy from within.

"Electricity in the bloodstream," he said, feeling totally strung out, jitters running through his veins.

"You reckon this food will calm me down?" he asked the kettle. It said nothing, but it was hardly impartial; it ran on electricity, too.

"I'm mostly water, you know," he said, trying to build a rapport. "We could be friends."

But the kettle wasn't made of water itself. It was stupid, stupid plastic. It held water hostage, tortured it, heating it like those rats trapped with nowhere to go but to burrow into the gory guts of screaming prisoners.

He heard the vermin scrambling in the walls again, eating through the timbers like they were the entrails of the house. Something stirred in his own guts and Marc farted loudly. The sound must have startled the rats, because they stopped moving. The toaster popped.

His bread, like his mind, was thoroughly cooked.

***

Burnt offerings; I am your God and you will sacrifice them to me.

***

Marc took the toast and even more coffee back into the office, and sat down to write. With eyes closed he saw the monster approaching an island. He felt a rush of curious exhilaration because there were tiny figures on the beach: humans.

With the omnipotent sight of the narrator he zoomed across to them. The island people had come out to offer their worship and sacrifices to the colossal beast wading out of the ocean. Marc was able to make out their individual faces, how this person was old and wrinkled, and another one young and vibrant. Here were women,

men, children; some tall and strong, others weak and hunched, all types. Their features were very specific yet somehow vague in his mind's eye.

On the beach—alongside their offerings of meat, vegetables, flower, and shells—they had spelled out in large rocks a word in English, all capitals: GODRISAUR.

Marc opened his eyes.

"How do they know the beast is called Godrisaur?" he asked himself.

Because you know Godrisaur, replied his mind, seemingly speaking of its own accord. Marc turned in his seat as if a voice had whispered over his shoulder, which is what it had felt like. But the voice was not behind him, it was in him, speaking with his own voice like a demonic Trojan horse.

"So these people are just extensions of me?" he asked.

The world held a mirror up to itself and created what could destroy it, the monster. And you did the same. These words you hear are that reflection in the pool of the soul. Each person who sees this mirrored image will look into the still waters of their own soul and see something, someone there. And in each act of creation they will insert themselves in this story. It is by their own will that they place themselves in the path of destruction.

As if a cold hand was closing the eyes of a deceased person, Marc felt icy fingers on his eyelids, forcing them down like doorways slamming shut…or coffin lids closing. In the darkness which followed, colors appeared, painting an image once more of the beach with its people, as well as the titanic monster out to sea.

It was huge, gigantic, monstrous—a leviathan from the deep, a behemoth born of nightmares, so large as to eclipse the sun and burden the horizon with its weight. Where it stole the sun's warmth and light it provided its own, the scaly hide dark and burned like baked earth, but through the cracks around each scale glowed a shining light, the red orange illumination of the inner Earth. Beyond its teeth blazed something brighter still, not red and orange but white and yellow, like it had bitten a chunk of the sun out of the sky and was now chewing on it, ingesting its power.

Marc picked up his toast without turning from the computer screen and took a big bite, his jaws working noisy and mechanically, the desire to feed unconscious, natural, necessary, but without focus or malice. He consumed so he may live.

***

My hunger! My need for living flesh fills my mind. I am Godrisaur, God eater, and mankind is made in God's image. I bend my vast body, an impossibly tall skyscraper folding in half. As my shadow stoops, it reveals the sun, haloing my monstrous head, and the worshippers on the beach fall to their knees at this brilliant display of my holy power. They, too, bend—though in submission where I do so in domination—offering themselves up to me.

I ignore the pitiful gifts they have laid out for me, the colorful bursts of flowers and sickly sweet fruits. I have no need for their shells piled like a dragon's hoard of gold. Even the proffered cuts of meat are nothing to me because they are already dead, and I need to consume life.

I eat people—miniature Gods—like totem statues placed here to idolize me, made in the image of the Anathema, that which I mirror. The cycle of creation and destruction is one circle, never ending.

Only with the ending of human life may I feel refreshed, reinvigorated. Not by the blood itself, not by the body, but by the soul animating the body. It is this I take from them as their lives are scooped up in my mouth. There they are burnt in the blazing heat of my power, the fire of my throat, and cast into a flaming abyss. In the depths of my being they will be consumed and reborn in a hell unimaginable. I shall walk around with them inside me, their death an eternal torment for them from which there is no escape.

Or so I have been promised. But the promises come from the Anathema and cannot be trusted.

***

Marc munched on his toast, sipped his coffee, watching in fascination as Godrisaur stomped up the beach, all the islanders having disappeared down its gullet. To his surprise the monster began to bite down on the fabric of the island itself, cracking open a volcano with teeth the length of streets. Molten magma burst forth, oozing down the mountainside. With surprising delicacy, as if it were performing a sacred rite, Godrisaur dipped its head and supped at the stream of impossibly hot lava. As it straightened once more, the thick, viscous flow of molten rock dripped down its chin. For a moment, the monster resembled the volcano, the flow of lava carving a path through its skin, and there was illusion that Godrisaur was one with the island, an extension of it, a naturally formed feature, one born of pressure and forces just like the volcano itself. It was a mountain range, a tectonic plate forced to the surface by another pushing at it from below.

Why has it come now? Marc asked his mind, but for once it was silent, and he knew there was a clue in this silence.

"Because now is when it came," he said aloud. "It is a self-fulfilling prophecy. There is nothing more mysterious here than the periodic visitation of the Black Plague. This beast is a scourge on the world."

He watched as it waded back into the ocean on the far side of the island, slowing, submerging itself like a sinking continent, consumed by the waves. A vast cloud of hissing steam rose where it disappeared beneath the water. It left behind cooling lava on the surface, congealing there like blood across a wound.

Marc felt pain at this, like the beast had scarred the world itself with its passing. Only when he looked down from the computer screen did he see his hand, realize he'd been cutting into the skin of his arm with his fingernails. Dark blood flowed from the injury, but as he lifted his hand in shock and horror, he saw the fingers were stained a much brighter red. It was then that he suspected that there were two sides to this experience he was having, one of which he was aware of, and the other, though dancing across his mind in colorful shapes, was only dawning upon him like a fresh sun peering over the horizon.

In his mind's eye the sun set on the island with the end of a day as one was beginning in his own reality, dawn breaking across his house like a wooden club across his back. There was a brilliant spike of pain and light, both traveling too fast to register for long, both capable of reaching him over long distances in an instant.

It was clear to Marc that the monster was coming, and though it was as yet still far away, this was no comfort. The march of time was inexorable and death inevitable.

***

I chase the sun, though I am slower than it. It is a father God where I am still a child, freshly birthed, still learning as I take baby steps across the ocean floor. My belly filled, I am satiated for a time, and can watch with a growing sense of awe as the marine life swims past me. For the first time since my creation I see them as more than mere prey; they, too, are avatars of this world, tiny portions of it made manifest. They are the blood cells flowing through the bloodstream of the planets.

But this thought makes me realize what I am. I am a blood clot, something to impede. I am an immovable wall; nothing gets past unless I will it. But I am necessary, am I not? There is no worse fate than immortal life. To live forever is to be without change, and though I am mighty and my life stretches out before me like the eons of history, I would not want to be this way for all eternity. Even this early in my new manifestation I crave death, the time when I might finally consume the God, and become the God, be one with the God once more.

I chomp my jaws playfully at a shoal of fish, but let them pass unharmed through my teeth. The blazing star within me has been pushed down my throat and resides in my belly for now. It is busy torturing the tormented souls I consumed earlier. They are in hell, a blasted wasteland with a merciless, burning sun. No relief for them, no respite, only toil under the gaze of a single, fiery eye which hates them.

***

Marc looked out the window at the sun. It looked hot and far too bright, and he'd been up all night working. Reluctantly, because it was hard to stop once the inertia was built up from the speed of creativity, he slowed the pace of words spewing out of him, through the keyboard, and onto the screen. But once the process of stopping began it was quick. His fingers became heavy, his eyelids with them, and he dozed at his desk. The doorways to his soul, his eyes, shut, blotting out the sun, forgetting it for a time.

He needed sleep or he'd burn out.

4

There is no rest for me. I am a burning effigy of the Gods, a passionately delivered elegy to commemorate the fall of mankind. I am a voodoo doll, trailing real blood and guts as pins of sunlight pierce the flesh of the world.

***

Marc hadn't slept, though he took a break, food and masturbation his only solace, Jain off to work at the hospital after giving him a love dose like a sharp needle up the back of his brain stem. There, the reptile part of his brain relished these lusty, burning passion parcels, consuming them quickly like dopamine junk food.

***

Sharks pop into my open mouth like candy. And I eat them endlessly even though I am not hungry. I eat them because I am distressed and restless.

For all my great size, with my stride to encompass a town, the sun has gotten away from me. The blazing sky chariot is too fast even for one as swift as I, and it has left me in darkness, running over the horizon so that its light no longer filters hazily down through the water to me.

I can follow its afterglow though, invisible currents in the water marked by the passage of its heat. Stumbling along like a baby after a parent who has abandoned it, I have only the death of others to console me.

The sharks are committing unconscious suicide, entering what they think is a cave. I could bring my belly fire up, deter them with its phantom light, but that would only attract other, light-curious marine life.

I suppose I am doomed, or blessed, to kill even when I do not intend it. And while I could close my mouth, I'm not going to do that. Even the vast turbulent wake I create with the moving of my body throws all into chaos around me. Rocks are thrown around in the water, moving as if in slow motion through air. Shoals of fish pass and are battered out of their preferred orderly formations.

Life is putty. Everything is warped by my presence. But even one such as I was made, squeezed out of a volcanic fissure, deep in a trench of the ocean.

Lava oozed out of that crack to form a mass protrusion, the cooling liquid rock taking on a form; that's how it was with my birth and will be again at my death. Yet my eyes glow with the twinkle of a being which cannot be made or unmade. Only my body can be undone.

That is how it should be. My form is changeable, mutable like the seasons. But my essence cannot be destroyed.

I will never cease to be.

I will only cease to be *here*.

***

Marc shuddered, feeling a presence looming over him like a lamp casting a shadow. Those shadows danced in his mind, moving fingers casting weird, psychotic silhouettes. He saw a world at war with itself, man against man, country against country, and all the senseless violence that accompanies bigotry. The shadows were liquid, flowing from one shape to the next, but all the while there were spatters of blood accumulating at the edge of his vision like dirt caught in his eyes. He blinked away tears; his own pain, the pain of others.

And this is even without the monster. This is the everyday world, the one we've been part of since the start of history and even beyond. Civil strife, holy war, murder... What could Godrisaur even add to such a terrible state of affairs? What fresh hell could it visit upon me, upon us?

The shadow pressed down hard on Marc's shoulder, a physical weight.

"You're hurting me," he said to it, and to the world. It was as if a giant book had been opened, and all the atrocities of the past spilled out onto him. He could remember every single awful thing he had ever read, all the pages of history he had pored over. They were a load he could not carry, bearing him to the ground, an awful burden, too much for one man to hold.

He was pressed flat on his back, staring up at a brown stain on the ceiling, unable to rise from the floor. In that stain he saw the guts of the universe sliced open and spread out for him to inspect as if they were a divine augury and he was reading the entrails of a sacrificed animal.

In that cosmic nothingness which represented everything, he saw a glimpse of something which gave him peace and forced a smile onto his face.

***

I am a monster. Do you think I don't know this? My question to you is this: do you know that you are a monster as well? If you aren't aware there is evil in you, I recommend you turn towards this darkness which dwells inside and examine it. I am not saying for a moment to give in to it. Not even I, with all my destructive power, give in to this darkness totally. I am more disciplined than that and retain in me a portion of light.

You can watch this black void rotate in your soul and find some peace in knowing you resist it, and on occasion do submit to its evil whims and desires.

***

"Is Godrisaur a bad thing?" Marc asked the cosmic kaleidoscope shifting above his sleep-deprived eyes with sparkling banality.

What do you mean by bad?

"Does it bring evil into the world? Does it hurt people?"

You know it does. But that does not make it bad.

"It doesn't? I would think those things are inherently bad."

There is no light without darkness. No life without death. No good without evil. Only with the option to do the opposite do we have any free will. Only through choice do we have any mechanism to exercise morality.

"We could have life without death, surely?"

No, life cannot exist in stagnation. Death is nothing but change and decay. Without it, there is no space for life to exist as a dynamic force, springing forth from recycled components.

"So Godrisaur is here to sweep away the old so the new might exist?"

Yes, Godrisaur is here to kill a God.

***

I am floating. I am an island surrounded by water. My body is cooling lava, forming the topography of a fresh landmass. Like all landmasses, my body is a living, dynamic thing. But instead of being rooted into the bedrock of the world, I am detached, a free agent. There is nothing beneath me but water, nothing above me but sky.

I am Godrisaur.

I am not an unthinking, unfeeling being. You have witnessed, though only in your imagination, a thousand different horrors. They burst forth like cackling demons, multiplying yet showing no differentiation. They are simply your fears made manifest.

I live. Despite bringing death, I am not dead myself. And though I have no soul, I can swallow souls. I feel them in my belly, writhing in agony, or else singing my praises, realizing, despite the pain, that they are being given an opportunity to grow. It is these souls I like best.

Life is not a bed of roses. It is not a source of pleasure. Only with entropy does anything grow. And only with growth does anything live. When it ceases to grow, I am there to cut away the dead parts, consume them, and turn them back into life.

But growth is difficult, so relish your pain, because it means you still live.

This last thought trickles through my being down into my guts, instructing those with ears to listen. It gives the tormented souls some hope, and I want them to have hope, because their hope is my own. I am nothing without them. Through their accumulated feelings and desires I become something new and dynamic, an amalgam of many souls.

I blend them together to fuel my inner sun, that which is not a soul but feeds on souls. And with it, I can continue, despite the weight of the stars bearing down on me from the night sky.

I look up at them as I float on my back, my stomach a mountain, my head a peninsula, my arms and legs forming harbors in which gather aquatic creatures seeking shelter from the turbulent violence of the ocean.

For a while I am content and at peace watching those stars. Each one is a sun, and I know the burden of suns, so I cannot trick myself for long. But together, forming patterns, those twinkling dots tell a story, something I can interpret as the fable of the Gods I have come to consume.

They tell me of the myths of humans, of their dreams, and I close my own eyes and see through yours.

***

Marc opened his eyes. He saw the phantom of sparkling lights fade away. Blinking, he realized he actually fell asleep. A huge relief. The burden of exhaustion had taken him to the floor, and the weight of the world had kept him there, covered by a depressive blanket of soil. It was as if he'd been buried alive, and now he rose from his grave, refreshed and invigorated with new energy, though not the same one as powered him before. Gone was the manic burst which had carried him through the night, made him create what he had created. Now things would take a new turn. It was day outside.

He could live his life.

5

"Why does it have to be so cold?" said Marc, putting a flannel jacket on over his jumper. "I can't seem to get my hands to warm up." He went and found the brown fingerless gloves Jain said made him look like a homeless dog, as well as the raggedy old black scarf covered in white pilling. Inspecting the ensemble in the wardrobe mirror, he said, "Well, I'm not winning any beauty contests."

Not that it was so cold outside in the sun. Australian houses were weird like that. They didn't really provide any warmth, just kind of kept the rain off and provided some shade in the summer.

"We're not really set up for winter," he said, but there was a heater in the living room, a rarity he'd never had in any of his previous homes. He considered turning it on, but then remembered the electricity bill. "I'm a writer, it's not like I have a bloody job to afford anything."

But Jain does.

"And Jain uses it when it's really cold. I could always go for a walk in the sun to warm up, but I've already bothered to put on these extra layers, and I have writing to do."

The prospect seemed harder now—writing—because he'd had some sleep, and with light coming through the windows, the world seemed not such a terrible place. There was nothing to fuel his manic energy, give that special horrible tinge to all stimuli. These were the tools of the horror author.

Yet he knew the monster was still out there, and, for some reason he didn't understand, it liked the sun, was drawn to it. So it wasn't so much the night to be feared, but the day. The sun was a lure, drawing the monster forever westward as it traveled around the world in an arc.

Marc went outside to the backyard, felt the sun on his face, and it warmed him.

But spend too long and the same sun burns.

He looked over the back fence. Trees, near and far, spread out over a grassy paddock sparsely populated with cows. These peaceful land-ships of meat took slow, meandering steps as they munched meditatively on the grass. Birds sang and chased each other through the air. It all seemed so idyllic, the fear of the night so far away. But, turning to the east, Marc could hear the roar of the ocean waves crashing, and this roar was like that of a great, monstrous beast.

A cat prowled in the long grass of the paddock, stalking some as yet unseen prey. It was closing in for the kill.

Godrisaur is coming, Marc thought, and went inside to record his impressions. Soon, too soon, he'd have to go to the beach, look at that roaring ocean and hear it more clearly, discern its meaning.

It spoke the words of a terrible God.

It was the death-knell of a civilization, ringing in his ears. As he entered the house and closed the door behind him, the sound didn't diminish. It stuck with him like tinnitus, driving him slowly mad, a screw being turned, boring into his brain with a high-pitched whine.

The whine repeated like an echo, this time outside of his head, and he looked down at the base of the glass door. The cat was there, meowing. This was the sound he heard. It was a far cry from the horrifying roar of a monster.

"To a bird or a rat, you're as much a harbinger of doom and destruction, though, aren't you?" he said to the cat as it scratched playfully at the glass.

He slid the door open. The cat meowed its gratitude, slinking through the gap. Marc bent down to pat the soft fur. It flowed smoothly through his hand like a feather boa as the cat tried to slide past without giving up the pats.

"Come on, I'd like a proper pat please, Kit Kat," he said, walking after the feline as it explored each room of the house in turn. Jain had dubbed the animal Kit Kat early on, when it wouldn't have a bar of them, and these visits were a distant dream they projected onto the aloof creature. Months of careful cultivation of the friendship had eventually brought the neighborhood cat to their door. Now it called on them daily, came inside, ritualistically visited each of the rooms, like a shaman in the form of an animal totem, cleansing the place of bad spirits.

Or simply marking his territory.

It was still hard to think of the cat as a male. Kit Kat was so beautiful and fluffy, long grey fur with a dignified white ruffle on the chest, white features on the face, and delicate, soft little white mitten paws. Marc's first names for him had been 'Princess Meow Meow' and 'Sunshine Kitty,' which both sounded unnecessarily feminine, almost insulting.

"Especially because I've seen you fight, haven't I?" he said to the cat at it pounced in among Jain's clothes in the open wardrobe, disappearing into the darkness. With tearing screeches and hissing scratches, Kit Kat regularly kicked the shit out of the neighbor's cat, something which gave Marc a sense of satisfaction, as that cat had never given him the time of day. When Kit Kat was prowling along the top of his back fence he was actually marking his territory and expanding it into the yard next door, not hunting birds but stalking a rival male in anticipation of a dust-up.

"We're all at war, aren't we?" said Marc. "That's the way of nature, not peaceful harmony. And humans are just animals in this regard, all of us trying to carve out a piece of land for our use, or secure sex and money."

But we need an antagonist. We need something to fight against to test our strength, to reveal our character. Only through adversity do we learn who we really are.

"Is that what Godrisaur is to me, a challenge, a trial by fire?"

***

Still floating on my back, still an artificial island, I open my massive jaws and regurgitate the sun from my belly. Sick of birds landing on me, sick of their stinking white shit covering my scales like some lonely, rocky outpost in the middle of the ocean, I let loose a burning cascade of fire, spewing forth lava in imitation of an erupting volcano. The night is lit up as the birds are consumed in flame, thousands of tiny fireballs quickly burning themselves out in the sky. Darkness returns, broken only by the wan moon, the twinkle of the stars, and the soft orange glow of my scales.

***

Consumed with burning thoughts of the monster, Marc was startled as Kit Kat jumped back out of the wardrobe.

"I forgot you were there in the shadows," he said to the cat, smiling to try to defuse his spiked nerves. "I used to wonder how you ever caught the birds, given they could fly away, but I can see now you catch them completely unawares. Just when they think they are safe, you are there to prove them otherwise."

A wave of sadness swept over Marc. Life was so good lately. Jain and he had entered a new realm of bliss in their relationship. They had a nice home they could afford, enough to eat. Both of them were years sober after struggling with addictions, and things were finally starting to settle down.

"I'm the bird, aren't I?" he said to Kit Kat, who just meowed in affirmation and left.

***

I rock my head back and forth contentedly as silken black ash—all that remains of a vast flock of birds—wafts slowly over my monstrous body like a light covering of tainted snow. A massively long tongue creeps from between my lips and slowly and methodically licks up these charred remains, these burnt offerings. Drawing them back into my mouth I swallow, gulping them down like a satisfying elixir; the very stuff of life transformed into death and back into life once more, the circle of predator and prey.

***

"I have to eat," said Marc, opening the fridge. For a second, he got a flash of a vision where the fridge was full of bloody cuts of meat. He recoiled in horror, slammed the door shut, but not before the vision disappeared, so he knew his vegetarian food would be there once more when he opened it again.

He took several deep breaths, and said, "I don't judge other people for eating meat. If they want to eat animals that's fine, but it's not for me."

Opening the fridge, the vegetables looked like the dismembered heads and limbs of their plant bodies, and he was horrified that we all had to kill *something* to continue to live.

"It must be an awful way to die though, to be food for some larger beast, consumed as a single meal to sustain them for a day, or maybe just a few hours. And it doesn't even end with your own bloody demise. Soon enough, hunger drives them to kill again."

Is that what serial killers feel, an insatiable hunger?

Marc bent down and pulled a head of cauliflower from the crisper. He weighed it in his hands, felt its heft. Turning it, he suspected that on its far side he'd see an accusing face. But there was nothing there, just more cauliflower, bland and uninteresting, happily lacking in horror. But the more he held it, the more he was weighed down by his need to eat, and he felt some envy for the dead, with their release from this burden.

***

Though I am forever, I am not always manifest in this realm. When I sleep in the bowels of the world I am small, I am nothing, and my needs are small, they are nothing. It is a blessed relief.

But this is not the way of things now. Now I am a living fire. I need fuel.

I must consume.

***

Marc turned on the stovetop, thinking once again of the electricity he was using and its cost.

"Better than having to go out and get firewood, though, I suppose," he said.

There had been a time in his life when this was necessary, when he'd lived in a cabin with a potbelly stove for heat, cooking on its cast iron top to make the best use of the limited fuel. It all seemed so primitive now, but also peaceful and full of rustic charm. It was a more tactile and immersive experience.

As he pulled a pan from the cupboard the electric stovetop glowed red, and he mused on the fact that this wasn't because the element was hot, per se, but to *warn* people that the element was hot using red light. It was a simulation, something to trick the brain into believing that we're still living, still connected with the ancient campfire, the source of mankind's power. It lit his imagination, cooked his meals. It fueled his ascent to the top of the food chain.

"Top of the food chain no longer," he said, placing the pan on the stovetop. He knew the red lights beneath went off when he did this, because they were no longer needed for the illusion. Wisps of smoky steam rose from the pan as heat infused it. He sprayed it with aerosol oil from a can—real oil was too expensive, and not as convenient—and picked up an egg.

He looked at it accusingly, feeling like a hypocrite. Wasn't there flesh inside this egg, the potential of a life torn away by his hunger? Was he a predator after all? He cracked it on the side of the pan and the yellow and white sizzled as they congealed and cooked.

"But this is the only thing connecting me to actual life anymore."

How else will I taste the Gods in a civilization so disconnected from the elements? Not even my fire is real.

But an elemental force was coming. In the Pacific Ocean Godrisaur rolled over.

6

The lack of sleep was catching up with Marc again. Not only was the screen of his computer sparkling disconcertingly, these points of dancing light were jumping from the screen into the air, spinning around his head and inducing a sense of dislocating vertigo.

He felt like he was being twisted around and around, the sparkles becoming fixed stars and he a planet at their center, rotating on his axis, the chair he sat on swiveling yet not swiveling, so that it was impossible to tell what was moving and what was stationary.

***

Metal birds circle me, shitting their explosive projectiles onto me. They spit in my face with bullets as they dive past me, cracking the air with supersonic whips. They are trying to corral me, contain me like cattle, for I suspect they know they cannot destroy me, their weapons useless. Even as their missiles streak in, blow chunks from my flesh, the exposed lava beneath the scales glows hot and cools in contact with the air, forming new rocky flesh, even more impervious to damage.

Still the human jets harass me, buzzing by my head like flies. At first, I do little more than shoo them away. In doing so, despite not even trying, I swat some from the sky, and I realize they are stupider and slower than flies. They erupt in fiery starbursts, flashing before my eyes in many colors.

***

It was like looking into a kaleidoscope, such was the intensity and variation of the colors and shapes which assaulted Marc's vision. He felt a headache forming behind his eyes. He'd been working too long and too hard. He had to stop. But he couldn't stop, whipped into frenzy, his mind spinning endlessly, not with ideas, but with pure, unidentifiable thought. It was as if he was witnessing the primordial soup of consciousness being stirred by a frustrated God. Seeking to cook something delicious and fresh, they instead were preparing nothing but yet another unpalatable poison.

***

Eat it. Eat the poison. I am the poison. I am Godrisaur. You are the God.

***

Marc tried to fix onto anything to stop the blurred movement. Unfortunately, his sight landed upon the dozens of paint pots on the edge of his desk.

Eat the poison. Drink the paint.

"How about a coffee?" he suggested, but the thought of more coffee made him feel even sicker than he already did, the dizziness almost overwhelming. He reached for the paint pots like a drowning man would a life raft. Grasping one in trembling fingers, he fought to open the lid, spilling a lot of the paint on the rug—

Jain's rug. She'll be so mad.

—in the process, but managed to get the rest to his lips. Tipping it back, it tasted bitter and sweet at the same time, a chemical tang mixed with a toxic sugariness. He licked his lips as the room started to slow a little in its relentless spinning.

The Earth is always spinning. You've only just begun to notice.

And while it didn't come to a complete halt, it at least became bearable. He put the paint pot down, noticing for the first time that the paint had no color. It wasn't that it was black, or white, or even grey, but that it was neutral, pure nothingness. Or perhaps it was all colors at once, and they had overloaded his senses so he couldn't read the colors individually, couldn't differentiate them.

This is what a rainbow must look like before it splits into the color spectrum.

"This is what the sky looks like before we interpret it as blue."

***

But the sky is black, and the ocean is black, and the hearts of men are black. It is night where I am, not day, and I see nothing but the ending of life, writ large in the explosive deaths of the pilots in their planes as I strike them from the sky. They are like words I cannot read, communication from the Anathema.

But I am not listening. I am killing.

***

Marc felt the circular motion pull at him like the tug of G-force. He blinked away that nothing color, saw it had become black, punctuated by fiery wounds, as if some great beast was stabbing through the fabric of the night sky, which is exactly what he was witnessing.

He was in the cockpit of a fighter jet, making an attack run on Godrisaur. Despite the darkness, he got his first good look at the thing, for it was lit up with explosions from weapons, and explosions from other fighters, knocked out of the sky, but also by the glow of its own flesh, which surged like the contents of an eerie orange lava lamp. Lumps of hard rock, the scales of the beast, flowed across these like the tectonic plates of a planet. Arranged down its spine were craggy mountains oozing magma from their tips, pointing down towards a tail which disappeared into the ocean—boiling where it made contact—and leading up to a massive head which utterly dwarfed the tiny specks of the jets harassing it. They shot their weapons impotently into its raging red pair of eyes and into the dark pits of its ears either side of its head. But they avoided its chomping mouth, bright sunshine peeking through those working jaws, silhouetting teeth which could bore deeper into the Earth than mankind's longest drill bit. The head sat on a neck that wasn't a neck—such was its squat girth—and a chest equally powerful sprouted two truncated yet agile arms, like the arms of a dinosaur. The belly was a rolling set of hills and valleys, leading down to thighs and legs which were barely covered by the towering waves of the turbulent ocean.

All this Marc processed in the few seconds it took for his plane to shoot past it. Without thinking, he released rockets which stabbed at the monster like accusing fingers.

"What are you doing here?" he asked.

As if in response, Godrisaur pivoted and opened its mouth. The yellow and white light in its gullet was the roiling sun at the heart of a world. With a high-pitched sound like a screaming release of steam, it unleashed a burst of star energy, a powerful heat ray which immolated Marc and his plane instantly.

7

The sun was burning Marc as he ran through the streets of his town. It wasn't quick, not like the death he'd experienced in the cockpit of the plane, a moment of brightness and the end rushing towards him, followed by nothingness. This was a slow, torturous process, like he was a hunk of meat on a grill, marinating in his own juices as he sizzled and cooked.

He felt like a man running for his life, though he knew he could no longer escape the forces which were overtaking him. Godrisaur was making its way towards the coast of Australia, destroying everything in its path. At the end of that journey was himself. Or, at least, it was the end of the journey as far as Marc was concerned.

When I die the whole world seems to die with me, because I myself know no more of it, he thought, taking the corner and jogging onto the path that ran through the park near his house.

His anxiety peaked, and his breathing was labored beyond the exertion of the run. He slowed to a trot, not willing to stop yet, thinking there was some chance that if he just kept going there was a means to escape it all. But there was no running from his fate, and certainly no running from anxiety.

The more he ran the worse it got. His heart beat harder, heavy like iron in his chest, and his lungs felt small and constricted. Each breath felt like he was sucking in fine needles that jabbed at his insides.

He looked around, seeking another path, but there was only the one he was on, with no other options, no way to turn. And turning around would only lead him back to where he started, with something terrible waiting for him there. Continuing on wasn't getting him anywhere, either. He would circle around the far side of the park and take the backstreets which linked up with the street he lived on. It would seem as if he'd run some distance, actually been some place, or obtained some destination. But he'd be back at his house again, staring at it, with the walls full of rats, and the horror of emotions waiting to dazzle him on his computer screen. And beyond both, on the horizon where the sun rose that day, now fading into a purple haze, a gigantic, monstrous head would soon peer over it like a serial killer peering over a windowsill.

He turned to look at the setting sun in the west. It was abandoning him, a last bright slash of a blade its legacy, leaving a blood red streak of sky.

The world was murdering him just as it had murdered this day. But was either of them ever going to last forever?

No. But there will be another day, not necessarily another me.

At least, he didn't think so.

***

I am not the first of my kind. I will not be the last. My conscious awareness of these past and future lives is limited. Though I have a mind, I am still a body, with many unconscious forces working within it which have more willpower than my mind could ever overcome.

The largest force is my hunger, but there are many others, not least the one which drags me after the sun. It is as if there is a magnetic lodestone in my brain, pointing always towards this blazing beacon. I seek to return to it for reasons I do not understand.

What will happen when I reach it? What will happen when I kill and eat it?

***

Marc was walking in circles in his backyard, occasionally stopping to do a stretch, cooling down from his run. His panic had eventually subsided into the steady rhythm of the exercise, and now it was over, he felt more at peace. He felt on top, which was why he was looking at the cows in the back paddock with renewed interest.

There seems to be a hierarchy in the world, thought Marc. *Like some creatures are more important than others, same as certain people are, or, at least, they think they're more important than others. Human is an apex predator. Look at the way we've humbled these cows. They don't even seem to notice the fence. But it's a big paddock. Maybe they don't care.*

What paddock am I in? Where are the limitations on my movements, on my actions? We have cages we live in and cages around those cages. Societal expectations, family obligations, the need to eat, shit, and piss. Sexual desire and career ambitions, as well as the pursuit of comfort and the escape from pain; are these things I control or that control me?

Behind them all, driving them forward like a cattle prod, is money, of course, because it is seen as a gateway to all the others, the force which overcomes all other forces. But money can only compel other humans to accede to our whims. It means nothing to nature, to the beasts. We cannot buy our way back to the top of the food chain if some animal knocks us off that perch.

We cannot buy off Godrisaur, same as we cannot buy off death. It comes for king and peasant alike.

But maybe a king has a better chance than most, not least because they can shove the peasants in the beast's way. Then they can enjoy the dubious honor of being the last one consumed.

The last human alive, with no one to console them in their final moments, isolated on top of a pyramid. A sacrifice like any other, their guts opened to the sun's rays by the blade of fate.

It's all the same in the end, going full circle. History repeats, not getting anywhere, despite all our furious exertions.

I cannot outrun this, and even if I tried to run…

He looked at the cows and the fences once more.

"There's eventually nowhere else to go."

8

Why do you run from me, star of this world? My aim is to kill and consume you. I do not mean you harm.

Don't you know that we live forever? Surely one as powerful as you, who exists in a perpetual cycle, bringing dawn to follow the long night over and over, understands this?

Trudging forever westwards I cannot seem to catch you. If only I could pluck you from the sky, a sweet morsel to lighten the burden of my burning hunger. You would be honored to perform such a service. I have witnessed your cults, the humans who worship you. You enjoy sacrifice, the giving over of the flesh, the ending of life for a cause. Isn't this your own fate?

You will be reborn. You will live again inside my belly. Don't you see the bright light which already resides there? It has not died. It is not my slave either. It is my symbiote. We are Yin and Yang, existing in and around one another, flowing into each other. Do you think the moon can satisfy you the way I can?

I turn my head up, see that pale orb overhead. Its round, mirrored face casts a reflection of your light across the calmed sea. It shimmers on the water, the strokes of a paintbrush. I hate it because it is a fake, a shadow. It is a replica, a forgery. The moon is an imposter.

I look westward. There, I find no glimpse of you, star of this world, no twinkling glimmer of your approach. I spin around, to the north, east, south, back to the west, and see nothing. I spy no pink slit on the horizon, no opening womb to birth a new day. I no longer feel your heat in the water. You are a long-dead corpse. You are missing. I wail in frustrated grief.

Thrashing, and continuing to spin, I am desperate to catch some sign of your return. I whip the waters to froth. I churn the air into frenzy. A column of fish is thrown into the sky, a hollow tube in which I am the center.

***

Marc was back at his computer, once again watching the updated live feed of the weather reports. He was meant to be writing his book, but instead was distracted by the internet, as usual.

This isn't the same thing, he thought. *This is important.*

"They're reporting it as a cyclone. But I know it is Godrisaur," he said, and he felt his stomach drop.

Am I really accepting that the monster is real? That it's actually out there and not just in my mind?

"You saw it," he said.

"Saw what?" said Jain from the doorway of his office.

Marc nearly hit the roof as he sprung up out of his chair in surprise. His immediate response was to try to cover the screen, conceal the proof of Godrisaur from her. He wanted to protect her from the monster.

The monster which I am responsible for. I created it, didn't I? Or did the world create it? I'm not some all-powerful God, for Christ's sake!

"What are you hiding?" asked Jain, her face crinkling in worried suspicion. "Are you watching porn? I don't care if you watch porn."

Marc laughed nervously. She brushed his hands away from the screen.

"The weather?" she asked, even more puzzled. "Geez, I don't mean to kink shame, but that's out there."

Yes, it is out there, he thought. He could see Godrisaur's monstrous head in his mind, remembered its monstrous visage in the split second before it atomized him and his jet with that beam of energy.

"Looks gnarly, though," she said, reading the weather feed. "A cyclone…it's coming this way, too. Damn it, I don't want to have to deal with that shit. I have work to do."

"You just got home from work," he said, disappointed. He was hoping they might be able to spend some time together. He needed a bit of love, a bit of grounding. The lack of sleep had left him frazzled and jangly.

"Yeah, but I have my thesis to get to."

"You're working too hard. You need a rest."

"You're one to talk. Have you had any sleep? Up all night writing this book."

This distracted Marc for a moment and he got excited. "Yes, I've written a lot. See?" He minimized the weather feed, revealing the word document of the book.

"Wow, yeah, you've written heaps," she said, looking at the number of words in the bottom left of the screen. Marc looked at the number as well, which seemed to be increasing with every word Jain said.

"That's weird," he said, and noted the word count also went up when he talked.

"What's all this about people being eaten?" asked Jain.

"Oh," said Marc, hurriedly minimizing the document, "you're not meant to see that."

Behind that the screen was filled with porn.

"That's an impressive amount of open tabs," she said, her eyes scanning left to right, eyebrows raised.

"I'm a bit embarrassed," he said.

"Don't be. When I watch porn I like to deep dive, too. You have to search around, right? Find what gets you off."

She cupped his cock and balls with her hand. "My big horny monster."

He laughed, waggling his eyebrows up and down suggestively. She patted his chest, smiled.

"Not now, I have to work on my paper," she said.

"And I have to work on my book, I suppose," he said, a bit deflated.

She gave him a kiss. "You have fun, baby." Then she left, shutting the door behind her.

Marc sighed. He sat at his desk and didn't pull the word document back up. Instead he started clicking around the open porn tabs.

***

I have no lust. I do not procreate. I am free of this desire at least. I do not create life. I bring only death and destruction. I command wind and fire. I manipulate water. I rupture earth. I am all these things in one, and they bend to me like words bend to you.

***

"It's like some elemental force," Marc said to himself after his sexual desire had been satisfied. He was partially referring to this ravenous appetite—which he found hard to keep satiated for long—and partially to the weather system which he inspected on his screen once more.

Of course they can't announce to the world that there's a monster out there the size of a city, tall enough to walk along the ocean floor with its head out of the water. There would be widespread panic. But what are they going to do when it reaches the mainland? Godrisaur has already smashed its way through isolated Pacific islands without word getting out to the public, but that won't be the case if it gets to New Zealand or Australia. There'll be no hiding it then.

"But how can I really be sure it's coming this way?" he said, tapping the screen with his finger, coaxing the feed to update. It did, and the cyclone system advanced a step towards Australia's east coast.

It's heading here, or at least they're reporting it as such. I guess they can't lie about the pressure system the monster is generating. Too many people have weather equipment. But the world's governments, at least some of them, know it's really a monster that's generating that pressure spike. They know it's a threat, and they're actively trying to stop it.

"What nationality was that jet I was in?" he asked, trying to remember so he had a better idea of who it was exactly that was attacking the monster.

He closed his eyes. With a swirl of rushing vertigo, he was back in a jet, though a different one this time—the first destroyed by that energy beam—but even this changed each second, his mind's sight jumping from cockpit to cockpit, giving him a stream of information as he seemed to inhabit a series of different personalities.

One was Japanese, another American. There was a South Korean man and then a Chinese woman. Leapfrogging from one to another he was bombarded with a Tower of Babel's worth of languages as the pilots and navigators spoke to each other and their commanders. What surprised Marc was that he could understand them all. Either that or, and this was perhaps more likely, he was inventing what they were saying himself.

He also heard their thoughts. Where their outward speech was terse and professional, though with a definite sense of strain, the words in their minds, their personal thoughts, were of awe, disbelief, and barely contained terror.

What is that thing?

It wiped out that whole squadron with a flick of its arm!

How are we meant to kill something so huge?

I'm never going to see my family again…

That last thought, which, like all the others, Marc heard in his own mind but with someone else's voice, hit especially hard. Marc thought of Jain and his parents, of losing them, and it was almost too much to bear. It choked him up and pulled him back to reality, where he sat in a chair and started to sob.

There was something bittersweet in his tears, because he remembered all those brave men and women in those planes, who were probably going to die horribly in the next few moments but still continued on despite impossible odds. Their families would grieve them just as he was imagining the loss of his loved ones and letting grief get the best of him. But they would be heroes, and he admired the way they confronted death with stoic courage, despite their internal fears.

It seemed the entire world had come together to fight this monster, and this was what Marc found so touching about the whole thing, that nations could put aside their differences and fight for life, fight to survive.

He just hoped it would be enough to overcome what they faced.

***

It is never enough! I crave more, more destruction, more death! The humans burst upon me like waves upon a shore. They are nothing against my will, against my power. I unleash the fury of the winds to knock them from the sky. I flex my muscles and they submit. I wade through their blood, flowing in a mighty torrent to stain the ocean red.

I feel the pressure pressing down from the air above, coursing through me like an electrical current as it descends down my body. It spreads out at the base of my feet like the roots of a tree. Each of these roots is a tendril from which new trees grow, encircling me in an invisible forest of power as they reach up, bending at their tips like bowing courtiers. This flow of energy is the Torus of the Gods. It is a perfect circle, a cycle of power. It is my gift, given freely, from one God to another.

I smash and purge all who come close, and I make a promise to those still far away: I am coming for you, too.

***

Marc was still sobbing, but this time it was not for those he cared about, or for those fighting Godrisaur.

He was crying for himself.

The beast would never stop until it killed him. Even then it would not be satisfied. And there was no way to destroy it, not now he had given it life. Godrisaur wasn't a phantom. It would not fade because he wasn't around to imagine it, to give it life. It would be reborn in the minds of the people who read his book. They would see it in their imaginations and thus make it real. As soon as they saw it, then Godrisaur would see them, too.

Then it would come to kill them as well.

***

Yes, you are already dead. It merely takes time, but death is coming for you. I am infinite. My will is ancient even though my incarnation is fresh. I can wait as long as it takes to see you become the corpse you already are.

You will die one day.

I will bear witness to that day.

9

"Are you crying?" asked Jain through the closed door. She gave it a little tap, seeking permission to enter, which she granted herself and came in.

Marc made a hurried attempt to brush away the tears, yet he still responded, "Yes."

"What's the matter, baby?"

"Oh, I don't know."

She hugged his head, held it close to her chest. "You're so exhausted. Is a book really worth all this?"

"There's obviously something wrong with me," he said, muffled by her breasts. "I try to take it easy, and then the book doesn't get written. Constant distractions, I can't get anything done. But then I focus, I go too hard and get worked up into a manic state. I get a lot done, but I burn out really quickly."

"You need to find a way to pace yourself."

"I just told you, I don't know how to do that. At least, how to do it and still get any work done."

"You had a plan, remember? Get up every morning and put in an hour or two before you get yourself into a state. Better that than making a big deal out of it, waiting all day and beating yourself up about it."

"Yeah, an hour or two gets some stuff done, chips away at it. But I can never stick to it. There's always too much anxiety and I need to work out or something else to get rid of the excess energy first."

"What's this book about, anyway?"

"I don't want to tell you. You'll worry."

"Okay, well, you can't say that and expect me not to worry. Now you *have* to tell me."

Marc couldn't bring himself to describe Godrisaur. Not yet. So, instead, he talked about what Godrisaur represented to him. "It's about the manic states I get into, the way they fill me with Godlike euphoria, yet simultaneously destroy things around me."

"Oh, okay. Yeah, I do get worried when you're like this."

"And it's also about reincarnation, as well as life and death, the stars, the sun, and the moon, light and darkness, Yin and Yang, duality."

"Sounds like a lot of Marc sort of things," she said, turning him gently in his chair and sitting on his lap. "I want you to stop for the night now. I want you to go and try to get some sleep. Maybe you'll dream about your book, get some new ideas."

The thought made Marc shudder, already seeing Godrisaur there in his dreams waiting for him. But it would feel good to rest his eyes, which were so tired they stung.

"Okay," he said, hugging her tightly. She felt warm, comforting. Her vitality and life reassured him everything would be alright. "It's time to put this to rest for a while."

***

In his dreams Marc did not see Godrisaur, but graves. They were peaceful things, cold slabs of stone and concrete, totally inert.

I guess that's why people put flowers on graves, to make them seem alive, to bring a sense of color and vitality to them. Maybe they're a promise of a resurrection, because the flowers always die, until next spring, when they return.

It is a cycle.

But do I ever come back? That stone looks pretty heavy, pretty permanent. It looks like it could weigh me down. If they tied it to my feet and dropped me in the ocean, I bet it could take me all the way to the bottom.

And what would I find there, darkness or a new kind of light? What do those deep sea fish see with their lanterns hanging before their faces? Not very much, I suppose, just a tiny circle, a small world. Wouldn't it be better to simply be blind?

I don't want to see anymore. I don't want to see what the future holds. Our deaths are inevitable.

But perhaps our resurrection is just as inevitable. If Godrisaur can come again, surely the young Gods of humanity could rise from the grave once more.

***

I am banging my monstrous fists on the ocean's surface in frustration. As quickly as I destroy the stinging metal insects the humans send against me, they send more. These flashing shapes come at me from the air and across the water. They even attack me from *within* the water. I can feel explosions tickling my toes beneath the waves. Looking down, I see silhouettes like whales darting about, birthing smaller versions of themselves which burrow through the water in their attempts to reach me.

Unleashing a bright beam of sun energy from my mouth, I turn the water to vapor, opening a vast chasm of empty space before me. With nowhere to hide, no medium through which to travel, the humans' black metal tubes clang to the bottom of the ocean, crumpled like tin cans, the larger ones with their smaller kin scattered around them like discarded toys. I stride forward and crush them flat for good measure, annoyed by their devious tactics and the itching sensation they have inflicted upon my legs.

Now they are dead, having achieved nothing but to have slowed me down. But this is enough to infuriate me, because I pursue the bright, swift sun. I cannot afford delay. These petty humans with their pinprick assaults cannot harm me, only form a stumbling block.

I must completely ignore them. But when I do this, striding forward with renewed purpose, their fliers buzz around my head, shoot directly into my eyes and ears. The blinding flashes and deafening ringing of these explosions are enough to drive me to madness. My mind is overwhelmed, my senses dazzled. I thrash about, but this increases my confusion. Everything is swirling about me.

The elements respond to the chaos I project, the wind circling one way around me and then reversing, clockwise and counter-clockwise in turn. The force of these winds shreds the planes to confetti, scattering their pieces far and wide. It also lifts the sea, ripping it up from its bed and hurling it in all directions. I stumble forward on what is temporarily dry ground, the seabed a scattered mess of marine life now beached in the middle of a huge ocean. They smear beneath my feet in rainbow gore, a colorful abstract artwork which no one can interpret. Shaking my head to clear the ringing, my sight returns, and I can make out little of what is around me. I wait for the compass in my head to stop spinning so I might get my bearings, continue on the path to my destiny.

Another human fleet, waiting beyond the horizon where the ocean still remains, flees before me. But I can sense further fleets of craft all around me, their looming presence like eyes watching from beyond the shadows of the night. They are coming from all over the world to confront me, to slow me down.

I stomp forward with renewed fury, desperate to hunt down my prey.

10

Marc woke up to the sound of Jain screaming.

"What? What is it?" he asked after he'd managed to tamp down an involuntary scream of his own.

It was bucketing rain and pitch dark in the bedroom. Jain murmured something through tears as he turned the bedside lamp on. It was hard to hear her over the torrential downpour striking the roof.

"What?" he repeated. "Christ, I can't believe how heavy the rain is."

A massive bang rocked the room, followed by another. For a second Marc thought it was the crack of very close lightning. But it happened again, a few times in quick succession, too clustered for lightning, and there was no flash of light through the curtains.

Jain pointed to the ceiling. "That!" she yelled.

They both jumped out of bed. Marc held Jain as they went down the corridor to the living room. They looked out the glass of the sliding door that led to their backyard. It was dark outside, the moon blotted out by what Marc could only assume were the rainclouds. He switched the back porch light on. Rain was falling so thickly it was as if God had dumped a bucket of water over the world. It didn't look like individual raindrops but a sheet of water, landing like a wave upon a beach.

"Are those fucking fish?" said Jain, pointing at the ground beyond the porch. Marc leaned forward to look. Flapping across the grass were dozens of fish. Some were a meter long, deep sea fish, but there were heaps of different types and sizes. It looked like someone had scooped up a portion of the ocean and tossed it over their house.

Then, just as quickly as it seemed to have started, the rain stopped, the noise stopped. The only sound was the frantic flapping of the fish as they drowned in the air.

"What the hell is happening?" said Jain as she opened the door.

"Don't go out there, not yet. We don't know what else might be dumped out of the sky."

"What do you think this is?" she said, watching the fish die, helpless to help them.

"Probably that cyclone picked them up, flung them far and wide."

"Seems possible, but how do you explain that?"

She dashed forward into the yard before he could prevent her. Skirting the piles of fish nimbly, she pointed over the back fence. The light of the moon shone there, and Marc looked up into the sky and realized there was no rainclouds, that the moon had merely been blocked by the water and the fish temporarily.

He stepped out into the yard with wary trepidation, one eye on the sky, expecting a fish to fall on him any moment. He probably wouldn't see it coming though. And he was more at risk from the fish on the ground, which thrashed around, biting in desperation at his toes. Whether they wanted his help, or just one last morsel to feast on before they died, he couldn't tell. He had to jump back to avoid the slash of the razor sharp bill of a swordfish. The thing flopped after him, nearly skewering him through the ankle with the vicious point of the appendage. The same fate nearly befell him as he accidentally stomped on a stingray. It whipped around with its barbed tail, leaving an angry red scrape on his skin, but it could have pierced right through his Achilles tendon. He darted aside, gave a few other aggressive fish a kick, punting each like a soccer ball, and reached Jain.

He expected a smartass comment out of her like, 'You certainly do have a way with animals,' or at least some concern for his wellbeing, but she was too busy dumbly pointing at the paddock over the fence. It was hard to tell exactly what they were looking at in the moonlight, but one thing was for sure—the cattle that lived in that field had suffered. Something which resembled twisted machinery had flattened more than a few into gory mounds of squashed flesh and shattered bone.

"Those poor buggers," said Marc.

"That looks like the wing of a plane, right?" said Jain, stabbing her finger at the closest hunk of sheared-through metal. She turned to him, her face a mask of disbelief. "Right?"

***

I must move forward. I must reach my destination. I can feel forces mustering to oppose me, and I will not suffer them lightly. The lodestone in my head rotates a few degrees. This confuses me for a moment before I realize the sun must be reaching the far side of the Earth. If I do not hurry it will escape forever into a new day.

With renewed vigor, I surge through the water, using my fat tail to propel me forward. Before me rises a bow wave to devastate coastlines, crush cities. I can feel it disrupt the fleets which are converging on my location. I am their sun; they seek me out. But I am not their prey, and neither are they mine. I am above them, moving with the celestial bodies, a manifestation of the Gods. I am a self-destruct mechanism in these immortal entities, clearing the way like a forest fire so that new growth may occur.

But the Gods do not go easily, because they forget they planted the seed of my creation deep in the bowels of the Earth. I have squeezed my way through rock, shifted my way through the substrata to make my way to the surface, and now I will be what I was born to be.

The hunter.

***

"Oh, God, what now?" said Jain, clinging to Marc.

There was a terrible, rushing roar on the wind. It was the cry of a behemoth, a world-ending shout of oblivion. It was abyss and void, the speech of a black hole.

And it was getting louder.

***

I open my mouth and unleash a torrent of noise to split the sky as hundreds of ships skirt my belly like a belt of stars twinkling in the moonlight. It is my voice, that of an ancient, primordial force unknown in the times of mankind.

***

Marc heard Godrisaur speak not with his ears, but in his mind. It was an alien sound, utterly devastating in both its intensity and strangeness. It was enough to drive a man mad, but he felt Jain's hand in his and this gave him the strength to open his eyes—he hadn't realized he was squeezing them shut—and escape from the realm of his imagination. There was still an awful sound, but it was a different one, like the ocean he heard every night in his bed, the waves crashing on the shore, yet much more intense, and rising to a higher pitch, like a colossal blade slicing through air.

***

"It's coming this way!" shrieked Jain, tugging at his arm, forcing him back towards the door. He didn't need much coaxing, but his curiosity made him stick to the spot for a moment. He saw something rising above the trees of the park which stood between them and the beach. It was a horizontal bar of white, with another bar of silver beneath it.

"It's a tsunami!" he said, turning to run back inside. He shoved Jain before him as she screamed. He was screaming, too.

They got inside the door as the wave smashed into the shore with a sound like an atomic bomb detonating. Seconds later their house was engulfed by rushing water. It swept the fish away, but also the fence and anything which wasn't bolted down.

"Get back from the windows," said Marc. Jain was frantic and he had to wrestle her into the central hallway of the house. Breaking glass and the whoosh of water bursting in followed. They were both wet up to their ankles, and then their knees, in seconds.

"How is this happening?" screamed Jain.

"Godrisaur!"

"God…*what?*"

***

The fleets of human battleships are pouring fire and brimstone upon me, but I am made of these substances, so I absorb their fury, make it part of me. They unleash hell, but I am hell. I grow larger still with each of their missiles, their high explosive shells. I open my mouth and gulp them down, happy they will at least be put to some useful purpose torturing those living souls I have swallowed. I hear the explosions go off in my belly, a faint glow shining through to my molten skin with each eruption of fire. I can hear screams, faint echoes of my own voice issuing from tiny throats.

You puny humans, you think you are the apex, the top of this world. But I am the apex, and I have come to humble you.

I take one last look at the flotilla of ships, the many hundreds of them gathered, the aircraft carriers, the cruisers, all the many escort craft; the Navy of a whole planet combined against me. I realize I am their Anathema, just as the creator sun is mine.

With this last bit of whimsy floating on my mind like a piece of flotsam and jetsam, I fall forward.

For a moment, they probably believe they have bested me, that I fall down dead. But no, I merely tire of them, and the rocky flab of my stomach crashes down into the water with explosive force. The ships are crushed instantly as I smash through the water's surface, displacing millions of tons of the stuff. It flies in all directions like the debris from an explosion, rushing out in gargantuan ripples to swallow small islands and devastate the coasts of continents.

I wallow for a second in this pond of disruption, pleased not only with the death I have wrought upon the ships, all the many thousands of lives ended, but with the deaths to come, the inevitable consequences of my actions spreading out across the Pacific Ocean to blight the lands of men.

11

"Look, I was going to tell you," Marc said to Jain as he waded through the water filling their house. The level had risen even more but seemed to have peaked for the moment. He made for the bedroom.

"Tell me what?" asked Jain, following after him. She tugged at his shirt. "Will you stop for a minute? What are you doing?"

"I'm going to pack."

"Pack?"

"Well, we can't stay here." He indicated the water with a vague wave of his hand.

Jain looked around as if noticing that their home was totaled for the very first time. "Oh, yeah, I suppose you're right. But where will we go?"

"Inland."

"But that wave of water, it's not going to happen again. We need to stay here and clean up. If we open the doors the water will flow out."

"You're wrong."

"Oh, okay," she said, crossing her arms with a huff. "I guess the water just lives with us now."

"I mean, there's going to be another wave, an even bigger one."

"Did it say that on those weather reports you've been obsessing over?"

"No, that's all propaganda." He pulled a suitcase down from the top of the wardrobe. "Here, hold this up out of the water."

She took it. "What are you talking about? Propaganda about the weather?"

"About Godrisaur," he said, and started taking some of their clothes from the wardrobe, putting them in the suitcase.

"Oh, yeah, you screamed that word before. I thought it was just some type of weird nerd cursing. Hey, can you stop picking my worst clothes?"

"If you don't like the way I pack, you do it."

"Are you nuts? Of course I want to pack."

"Well, okay, give me the suitcase then, but make sure you get my—"

"See? It's fucking annoying if someone doesn't get the right stuff." She quickly and efficiently put both their favorite clothes into the suitcase without another word from him, pre-empting every choice he would have made.

"You know me so well," he said, and she winked at him.

He grinned like an idiot. Even in this flooded house, disheveled and soaking wet from the tsunami, with her hair plastered to her head, she was the most beautiful woman he'd ever seen.

She zipped up the suitcase. "Yes, I do know you very well, better than anyone. So I don't think it's a stretch for me to assume that whatever this whole Godrisaur thing is, maybe it's a product of your recent lack of sleep and an overactive imagination."

"That's a bit dismissive and mean."

She gave him a significant look. He shrugged.

"Okay, there's something to that," he said. "But it's still real, okay? What do you think caused this inundation?"

"Umm, the cyclone," she said with a cocked eyebrow, "of course."

"The cyclone *is* Godrisaur!"

"So Godrisaur is the name of the cyclone?"

"What? No. The cyclone they're reporting, it's a cover to hide Godrisaur from the public. People would panic if they knew what Godrisaur really is."

"And what's that?"

He threw his hands up dramatically. "It's a Kaiju!"

"In English, please."

His hands dropped in disappointment, the drama lost. "A fuck off big monster," he deadpanned.

"Pfft, as if that's a thing," she said with a glib flick of her wrist.

"You saw the wave it caused, the fish falling from the sky. They were ocean fish, flung hundreds of kilometers through the air."

"That doesn't mean a monster did it, and it'd have to be pretty huge to have such an effect. It's not like something like that could hide. We'd all notice."

"People have. They've been weaving a web of fake news around it, disguising it as a natural event, which, I guess, isn't so far from the truth, really."

"You can't expect me to believe every cyclone has been a front for a monster…someone would have leaked the info."

"Not every cyclone, just this one. Godrisaur has been dormant for a long time, probably millennia."

"How could you possibly know that? And how do you know its name?"

"I think… Well, it's going to sound silly."

"Silly? You mean sillier, right?

Marc rubbed the back of his neck, looking down. "I think I had something to do with its creation."

"Okay, you can stop right there, because we've definitely crossed over into lack of sleep and too much coffee territory."

"It's in the book I'm writing."

"I thought you said it was about reincarnation."

"Yeah, the reincarnation of an ancient monster, come to kill us all."

"Marc, look at me." She took his head in her hands. "You're just really tired, and you're scaring me."

"*I'm* scaring you? Not the tidal wave that smacked our house? Not the monster that caused it?"

"The monster isn't real."

"It is."

"And what makes you so sure?"

"Because I can see it in my mind."

***

I am free. There are no barriers before me now. I glide forward like the ships I have crushed beneath my bulk, my tail working like a rotating propeller, thrusting me forward at terrific speed.

I chase after the colossal wave my dive into the water created. It smashes everything aside, announcing my approach like a herald, the trumpets of doom sounding as it crashes into islands which disappear beneath its smothering embrace.

But something is changing and the water beneath me becomes shallower. My feet reach out to touch the bottom. I rear up, erect at my full height, my head rising so high as to discern the curvature of the Earth. From this vantage point I can see the dark horizon, the stars a dazzling belt, girding the planet. Striding forward I emerge from the water, my monstrous clawed toes scouring the already devastated soil. There is nothing living there. The wave has scourged it, flattening all features into a muddy amorphous mass.

But while this landmass I stand on is larger than the others, it is still an island, and not a wide one. Just a few hundred kilometers distant, it disappears into the sea once more. This rock is nothing but a hurdle for me to step over. But as I do, I feel the mass of my brain rotate in my skull, turning to indicate back the way I have come. I see a light shining onto the ground beneath my feet, faint and pink, but becoming yellower each moment.

My whole body pulses in anticipation and panic, the scales of my skin expanding and contracting, oozing lava down my sides like the molten sweat of a planet.

The sun has returned. But I am not chasing it. It has turned the tables. It has become the hunter and I the prey. It has the drop on me.

I swing my bulky body around, my colossal tail sweeping a whole country into the sea, destroying anything the wave did not. All is death beneath me, squished flat. I do not care.

The light has come back into my life, a harbinger of doom. It slices the horizon as I squint off into the east. There the sun rises, a bloody dawn of red. It is a yellow slit like the vagina of space, opening up to admit the passage of a gore-covered child of light.

I hear its energy scream, its beams of sunshine stabbing impossibly fast to carve into my flesh.

But I am not beat yet. It will take more than this to overcome me.

I am still the hunter. I can lie in wait. I am tough as a mountain. I can weather your awful barrage of light. And when you are overhead, what then?

It is kill or be killed.

***

“We have to go!” Marc said to Jain, dragging her towards the front door.

“Stop,” she said, struggling, but his grip on her was tight. “You’re hurting me.”

“I don’t have time to explain, Jain. That second wave is coming, and it’s much bigger. Trust me, okay?”

"Look, can you stop for a second? I'm cold and wet, and really tired. I worked all day, you know?"

"I worked, too, and got less sleep."

"Oh, yeah, right, *work.*" She punctuated her sarcasm with inverted commas made with her fingers. "You just wrote your book, the one which magically creates monsters and natural disasters, apparently."

"You're usually not so dismissive of my work."

"I respect what you do, but this is a bit much, Marc."

"Whether I'm right or wrong about Godrisaur, or even if there is or isn't going to be another wave, it doesn't hurt to get to higher ground, right? Just in case."

She rolled her eyes. "Alright, but where are we going to go?"

"We'll go to my parents' place."

"Oh, no, Marc, they don't even have running water."

"They have running water. They just have it turned off most of the time."

"Semantics."

"I think you can agree water is something none of us are lacking at the moment." He splashed around in their living room.

"That's seawater. We can't drink that."

"All the more reason to go to their place. Do you know how many bottles of water they have filled up out there?"

"A lot."

"That's right, a lot. And we don't know if the utilities will be functioning."

As if on cue, the lights went off in their house.

"Damn," Marc said. "People are going to be panicking."

"That sounds like it's best to stay inside then."

"No, we need to get out of town. And we're not getting any drier or warmer here. Plus, we're right near the ocean. We're vulnerable here. Please, let's get inland a bit. They live up on a big hill. We've got a much better chance there. And I want to make sure they're alright."

"What about my family?" she asked, and immediately started fretting with her hands. "Damn it, I've only just thought of them. I'm a bad person. Marc, we have to go save my mother. And then there's my sisters, their kids, come on."

"They're too far away."

"It's driving distance."

He gave her an incredulous look. "You think we're taking the car?"

"Well, yeah, how are we getting to your folks' place?"

Marc jerked his head towards their garage, which didn't contain their car, which was parked on the street and would have certainly been totaled by the tsunami. It took Jain a moment to click as to his intention.

"We're going to ride bicycles?" she asked, incredulous, jaw dropping.

***

The sun cycles overhead, detouring from its passage around the Earth to make miniature orbits where I am the central point. The shining light of its movement forms a halo around my head. I do not know if this is a blessing or a curse. To a human, this would appear as a miracle. To me, it is merely another of the devious tricks of the Anathema.

For a long while I am mesmerized by the sun's circular motion, bedazzled by the proximity of its brilliance. The sunbeams shoot into my eyes, blinding me so all I see is bright darkness.

I flail with my arms, but I am weakened, my blows unguided and without power. My arms feel sluggish, as if dragging through a thick liquid. In a drugged stupor, I stumble, kicking the top off a mountain. I slip on the great slush pile of melted snow which slides from its peak.

Falling, I collide hard with the rock of the country beneath me, and, to my utter shock, there is *pain*.

***

"I know it hurts, but you have to leave them," said Jain. She was already on her bike and fiddling with the manual release mechanism on the garage door.

"I can't walk away. I can't abandon them," he said, tears in his eyes as he held them.

"They're toys!"

"They're collectible miniatures."

"The water has got in the boxes anyway. They're ruined."

"They're plastic. I don't care about the boxes."

"You do care about the boxes. I see you stacking them and talking to them."

"I like the art on the covers."

"Look, just pick your favorite one and let's go."

"Two, I'll take two."

She tugged on the red cord of the garage door, disabling the connection to the useless electrical chain-driven opening system. "You're lucky I'm letting you take one. You don't think I wouldn't like to go back for another pair of underwear or ten?"

"You can go back for another pair if I can take two miniatures."

"You're going to struggle with that suitcase enough as it is."

"Oh, yes, you're right. Maybe I should transfer everything into a backpack."

"No way, a backpack is too small. I've cut it down to as little of my clothes as I can bear."

"Well, you could get a backpack. What are you carrying?"

She rolled her eyes and bent awkwardly over from the seat of her bike, wrenching the garage door open manually. "I'm carrying the burden of your hare-brained scheme, riding a bike through a half flooded town up into the hills."

The sound of shouts and screams reached them immediately, with people running around in panic. Some were calling the names of lost relatives, some crying out in pain.

Others lay completely still, face down in the shallow water.

"Oh, God, we're not going to go out in that, are we?" Jain said, visibly recoiling from the sight.

"We have to," Marc said as he closed his eyes, eyelids fluttering, "Godrisaur's reached New Zealand."

Jain gave him a dubious look. "Surely we would have heard something if a giant monster was striding across New Zealand." She fished her phone out of a soggy pocket. "Not that I'm getting any signal."

He opened his eyes and looked at her. "The towers are probably down."

"I thought mobile phones worked on satellites."

"No, it's all undersea cables and towers."

"Are you sure?"

"If it were satellites the phone would work."

"I'm going to try calling my mother."

"Okay, but don't get your hopes up."

She held the phone to her ear. After a while, she lowered her arm. "Nothing, and don't you dare say I told you so."

"I'm not a monster."

"No, you only create them with your mind, apparently by the magical act of writing a book."

"Fuck!"

"What?"

"I forgot about the book." Marc ran back into the house, wading through the flooded rooms, and grabbed his laptop off his desk. He ran his hands over it, checking for moisture or damage. "Thank God it's alright."

"There's not room for your computer *and* miniatures," said Jain when he returned to the garage.

Marc swept the colorful boxes into the water. "Fuck the miniatures," he said, stuffing the laptop into the suitcase, which he balanced precariously on the handlebars as he mounted his bike. Inching out of the garage door, he peered left and right. "Okay, the coast is clear, let's go."

"What are you checking for?"

"It's the end of the world. We have to watch out. People are going to start acting crazy."

"Yeah, I'm aware," she said, giving him a sidelong glance.

***

I feel like I'm losing my mind. I am humbled by my insanity, lost in a world of shifting shapes without meaning. Blinded by a twisting kaleidoscope of colors, the sun beats me into submission. Each time I try to stand it blasts me with a wall of light, knocking me from my feet. It fills my eyeless sight with visions of my own destruction and I do not like it. I bring destruction, I *am* destruction, and while I know I must one day be folded back into the fabric of the Earth, I don't like being reminded there might be some end to this cycle of rebirth. It shows me what this would be like, to be reabsorbed into the white light of the Anathema. It is not the peace I seek at the end of a long journey, but a defeat, and I flee from it, flopping into the ocean. The water boils at the touch of my molten lava body. Hissing steam is thrown into the air in rising banks, forming clouds that momentarily obscure the sun.

I am able to open my eyes again, and I catch a glimpse of the sun's malevolent stare through this foggy haze. It is done with me, no longer my halo, but once again a father figure, fleeing from me, casting me away. I am unwanted, unloved. I reach out with my massive claws, beckoning it to return.

It has already rushed on, leaving me behind, with its light still reaching me, but fading, gone off to light another land, bless it with the dawn which ambushed me so successfully.

12

"Well, the sun is coming up at least. That's a positive," said Jain as the first light appeared on the horizon. It lit a bizarre scene of destruction and human misery, the town waterlogged and clogged with broken debris. Everywhere people were running about, wailing in panic, with very few trying to help the wounded, most others lost in their own misery and suffering. There were dead bodies, some being grieved over or pulled from the water. Others floated by, unloved, untended for, now just another piece of discarded rubbish in this hellish abyss.

"Maybe we should stay," said Jain, her face twisted with conflicting emotions.

"I told you, there's another, even bigger wave coming," said Marc, struggling to pedal his bike through the water that reached halfway up their wheels.

"Should we tell people, then?"

"How would we do that? And who exactly would listen?"

"There's another wave coming! Get to high ground!" shouted Jain to anyone within earshot.

It was no surprise to Marc that everyone ignored her, lost in their own wild shouts, their own warnings and calls for aid, all going unheeded in this chaotic mass of struggling humanity. The words were swept away as surely as their town was by the water.

A lot of buildings were still standing, even if fences and cars were carried away, piled high in ditches with all the miscellaneous debris of life which can be carted away in a moment by a disaster.

That will change with the second wave, thought Marc. *All these houses will be rubble, these people crushed and drowned, and us with them if we don't hurry.*

"Save your breath, Jain, we have to save ourselves. Think of your family. They want to see you again."

"Oh, God, my family," she said, choking up, the emotions heightened by her empathy for those suffering around her. She stopped pedaling, looked back at him. "Will I ever see them again?"

He gave her a shove in the back as he rode level with her, which nearly toppled him from his bike, and said, "If you live, there's a chance you will, but if you just lie down and die here, then there's no chance. Please, Jain, fight. You need to survive for me if not for yourself."

"Some of them are sure to die, though. It's just odds."

"Family members?" he asked, wrestling awkwardly with the suitcase, looking back the way they had come, back towards the ocean, with fear and trepidation in his wide eyes.

"Yeah, think for a second of everyone you care about. There's so many, it's just probability that some of them won't make it. But which ones will survive? Which ones would you choose to lose if you could pick?"

"We don't get to pick, though. It's out of our hands."

"Then who gets to pick?"

"I don't know, Jain, the Gods?"

"What a crushing burden of responsibility."

"Stop it. You don't have to think about all that. You just have to think about yourself. It's time to be selfish, dig deep and find some sense of self-preservation."

"I always told you if the apocalypse came I'd give up. Who wants to live in a world like that?"

"And?"

"I still want to live, Marc. I don't want to die like this."

He pushed her again. “Then put your feet on the pedals and ride!”

She didn’t say anything, but she did take off, faster this time, her feet working furiously to surge through the water. She finally had the adrenaline of fight or flight flowing in her.

“Hey, wait up!” said Marc, clumsily getting his own bike going, trying not to drop the suitcase in the water.

***

I can see again, and though the light is fading, I can tell there is something hidden over the horizon, a large mass of land, perhaps a whole continent. I feel the wave of destruction I created slamming into it, some of that force bouncing off and rebounding back towards me. It is a measure of time, a measure of death, like a sonar ping, like a blind bat or a singing dolphin.

I race to catch up with it, knowing there is something to eat waiting for me, a meal to satisfy not my hunger but my anger.

I need to feast on blood, to see life ended, to see other beings lose everything, if only to distract me from what I have lost myself.

***

“Will you look at that?” said Marc, stopping on the crest of the hill. He planted his feet either side of the bike and sloughed the heavy suitcase off onto dry ground. He pointed back down the fertile valley of sugarcane fields which led to the ocean.

“Fuck, you were right,” said Jain, jumping off her bike and letting it drop. Her eyes jumped from their sockets, her jaw dropping to the ground at the awe-inspiring spectacle of primordial fury they were witnessing.

A huge wave rose on the horizon like the walls of a colossal castle, crested with jagged battlements of furious white froth which sparkled with sunlight. The dawn sun itself seemed to ride the wave like a chariot mounted God, come to wreak a terrible vengeance. It had a good vantage point to view the apocalyptic destruction of humanity, the wiping of the slate clean.

Nature doesn't care if all of mankind is killed, thought Marc. *In time the crushing water and burning sunshine will nourish plants to grow through the cracks left by the ruin of our civilization. It won't take long for the world to be reclaimed, humans forgotten.*

"What's going to happen to us? What's going to happen to Australia?" asked Jain. She had to raise her voice above the deafening roar of the wave.

"Destruction," said Marc, the word punctuated by a massive, ear-splitting bang which made them flinch and reach for their ears. The tsunami wave, many times taller than the first, broke as it struck the coast. It folded in half and plunged straight down, gouging a huge chunk out of the continent, carrying millions of tons of soil away. Their town, just ten kilometers distant, went with it, thousands of people dragged to their doom, the wave sweeping them back into the ocean like a lucky gambler raking in their chips.

But the wave wasn't done. It had layers upon layers, elemental soldiers marching to the attack in packed ranks. As each successive one fell like a curtain it revealed another wave behind. Each one demanded its toll, paid in the precious lives of those who hadn't gotten clear like Marc and Jain. And each wave was greedy for land, hungrily gulping down kilometer after kilometer of farmlands, flooding them with water which tore at the soil in dreadful swells which ebbed and flowed across the valley like a scouring scythe.

Jain was dumbfounded, shaking her head in disbelief. Marc felt like he was going to be sick.

We could have easily been down there when that happened, he thought, but quickly corrected himself. *No, that was never going to be the case, because if I die, who will tell the story?*

***

Do you think you're so special? Do you think my mind flows from yours? What about the other ones, the ones who will picture me in their thoughts, what of them? You are not special. You can die. As long as one God remains I have a reason to continue.

But I will eat them as well. Then I can find the peace which eludes me.

Furiously, I swim on, seeking the beating heart. I will tear it from your chest and end your hubris once and for all.

13

Taking a break on a grassy ridge, Marc cut the fruit in two and bit into its flesh, the crimson juice running down his chin like blood. Sitting on a rock opposite him, Jain was similarly devouring a mushy brown fruit which smeared her lips like shit. Their panicked flight and the awe-inspiring destruction they had witnessed had given way to the mundanity of the need to eat, and Marc had raided a fruit-themed amusement park which overlooked the valley, trying to steer clear of any staff, but not seeing any. Now, sitting in the morning sun, it seemed like any other day, not the end of the world at all, but rather the intimate picnic of two lovers.

"These things always have such exotic names," he said, referring to the fruit. He was trying to change the topic from the ubiquitous one they had continued to slide into, that being, who from people they knew they thought was already dead based upon the geographic location of their house or apartment.

"What's mine called?" she said, holding up the brown skin, licking her fingers clean of the feces-like innards of the thing.

"Chocolate pudding fruit," he said. "Mine is a dragon fruit."

"I know what a dragon fruit is."

"You asked."

"Why do they call it a dragon fruit?"

"Oh, now you want to know about it?"

"You just seem to know something about everything."

"Ah, the author's curse—a little knowledge about everything, but an expert on nothing."

"So why's it called a dragon fruit?"

He handed her the skin, having finished hollowing out the tasty insides, his hands stained red like he'd carved the heart out of a sacrificial victim. "Looks like the skin of a dragon, doesn't it?"

"Yeah I suppose it does, one with pink and green scales. But I don't think that's the reason."

"Oh?"

"It looks like a fireball, right? If you hold it like this so the wavy green tips go up like licking flames, the pink now the fiery core. So the name could be because dragons breathe fire."

"Haven't heard that explanation before," he said, grabbing a fresh one from the bundle he'd picked off the plant's fat, spikey vines. He pretended to shoot it like a fireball from his palms, tossing it to her.

She caught it, juggling it like a hot potato.

"Ouch, ouch," she said, as if it was burning her fingers.

Marc laughed. Then Jain held the dragon fruit in her palm, inspected it like a crystal ball which could see not only the future, but some magical alternative reality.

"Wouldn't it be crazy if dragons were real?" she asked.

"Oh…" said Marc. He kicked the dirt with his foot. "Yeah, that *would* be crazy."

***

I open my mouth and unleash another torrent of fiery light energy to scorch the sky. The beam chases after the helicopters which swarm my head as I wade through the ocean. Their chopping rotors fill the air with a malignant hum which hurts my ears, and the constant explosions erupting around my face dazzle my eyes as they fire their weapons directly into them. Enraged, and blinking back magma tears, I keep spewing up energy, sweeping the brilliant spear of light back and forth blindly, taking out dozens of the swarming parasites. Yet still more hound me, seeking to confuse me and turn me off course.

But I have the lodestone in my head, which guides me on always…

Guides me towards you.

***

A shudder ran down Marc's spine.

"What is it?" asked Jain, smearing her dirty fingers on her pajamas, which were finally starting to dry off in the sun. Marc shivered again, and not from the cold, his own clothes no longer as damp as before.

"I think we need to keep going. I thought we just needed to get to high ground, but I've got a bad feeling," he said.

"Do you think there's another wave coming? We're pretty high on this ridge." Jain jumped up on a rock, looked left and right with a sweeping motion of her head to take in the entirety of the flooded valley. "We're better off than the people down there."

Marc got up beside her. He could just make out tiny figures in the distance, some in boats, others flailing their arms, either drowning or trying to draw attention. "Wow, I'm surprised anyone survived."

"Even Noah and his family survived the flooding of the whole world."

"Somehow along with two of every animal. That ship must have been cramped."

Jain's face dropped in sadness. "I don't think many animals will get out of that quagmire."

Marc pointed to a pair of butterflies fluttering past. "Life still goes on." He took her hand in his and they shared a smile, watching the butterflies dance around each other.

"He's certainly a randy guy," said Marc after a while, referring to the overly eager one chasing the other. "Hounding the poor girl."

"Oh, I know what that's like," said Jain, rolling her eyes.

Marc waggled his eyebrows at her suggestively. "How about it?"

"Didn't you just say we need to get going?"

"I'm never in that much of a hurry I'd turn down sex."

"Civilization is collapsing."

"Even more of a reason to get a root in."

She slapped away his groping hands. "Charming."

***

I smack one of the bigger helicopters out of the sky, its twin rotors careening in different directions with discordant whines as it is cleaved in two. This doesn't seem to discourage its companion craft, who come in close, taking more casualties as I swat them down one by one. They tumble into the sea in mangled heaps but still more come on. The fattest ones hover by my head, ropes tossed from their open bay doors. Tiny little figures clad in black like glossy-shelled beetles rappel down these to land on my shoulders.

I shake my body, sending a seismic tremor across my skin to slough them off. Some tumble to their doom in the ocean far below, but others cling tight as they drive spikes into my rocky flesh, fastening themselves to me. I'm offended by the presence of these parasitic humans, their impertinence in burrowing into my skin like ticks. I hate the impurity of having their base metals penetrating my body. Even if there is no pain or discomfort on my flesh itself, I can feel an effect in my mind, tingling at the base of my metallic brain. The lodestone there is turning;

they are deploying some type of technology to throw off my gyroscope. Weaving a current of electricity around my neck with thick wires they unspool, I realize they are trying to enslave me with a collar of superconducting metals to confuse my internal compass.

In a panic, seeing finally a real threat from these industrious insects, I expand my scales and heat the magma beneath the surface of my skin. It oozes forth like a thick secretion of fiery sweat, melting the humans into screaming pools of liquid gore in seconds.

But their work is done, and a current flows around and around my neck, girdling my thoughts like a cage. In my head, the lodestone spins like a moon in orbit around a central point in my brain. I feel a mounting sense of horror completely alien to me as my body follows suit and I stumble in a circle. The sun spins past my vision with each rotation I make, but I cannot lock onto it, my sight obscured as even larger helicopters blot it out like cataracts. Then I am truly blinded as massive spotlights mounted on the helicopters are activated. They flash on like the opening eyes of a God, their brilliant beams bright as the sun.

Now I see many stars, but which one is real? I don't know which way to turn, so I continue to spin.

***

The wheels of the bikes spun on the road as Marc and Jain pushed to cover the remaining distance along the ridges and hills to Marc's parents' house.

"My knees really hurt," said Jain. "And this seat is pounding me, and not in the good way."

Marc laughed, but Jain wasn't really in the mood for joking, as she scowled and slowed down.

"We've got to keep trying," said Marc. "I think the militaries of the world have bought us more time with some type of high tech ploy, but it's only temporary. Godrisaur will break free and Australia isn't ready."

"You'd think we'd be used to being terrorized by dangerous lizards by now," she said, putting on a brave face and pedaling a bit more.

Marc stopped. "Wait a second."

"I just got going I'm not stopping, thanks."

He pedaled up beside her. "You mentioned lizards. How do you know Godrisaur resembles a big reptile?"

"What? I don't know, you must have told me."

"No, I didn't. I said it's a big monster."

"I just assumed then."

"Can you…can you see it? When you close your eyes, can you see Godrisaur?"

"I'm trying to ride a bike, Marc."

"I'm not saying close your eyes, but can you visualize it, even though you've never seen it?"

"That's what *you* do, isn't it, when you write about it?"

"Yeah, but it's my book."

She sighed. "Look, I told you my knees really hurt."

"Perhaps, even though you haven't read the book, it gets in your head, too, because I'm telling you the story."

"We're living the fucking story, and it's not a pleasant one. Why didn't we bring any water? I'm so thirsty."

"There's a water bottle on the bike there."

"I forgot to fill it up before we left."

"Oh, mine has water. Here." He handed his bottle to her. She gulped the remainder down greedily.

"We might have needed to ration that, but alright," he said, taking back the empty bottle and replacing it on his bike. He pedaled on ahead of her as the trees either side of the road opened up onto empty space.

"You said we're nearly there," she whined.

"Oh, shit," he said, stopping. "I didn't take that into account, though."

"What now?"

She struggled with a few more pumps of her legs to reach him, and then came to a stop with a weary sigh. A ravine lay before them, a jagged gash in the earth between this ridge and the next.

And the bridge spanning the space had been swept away by the tsunami.

14

I have no way to bridge my present experience of confusion with my projected goal, my destiny. I seek to kill a God, yet I feel as if I have been slain myself. I am lost in an abyss of tangled sense perceptions. I am brutally aware of only one thing, that my own life and death, my rebirth and reabsorption into the world, is a cycle. This knowledge circles around and around my head, around my neck, like a noose.

My thoughts are charged electrons. They are mindless entropy. I lash out in furious abandon, but it does no good.

Nothing comes of all my energy, of all my attempts to humble the Anathema. I will return to whence I came, and it will continue spinning around this Earth, a star God, lord of its domain, and I, its humble servant, shall be cowed once more.

***

"That's it," said Jain, staring at the abyss before them, water running through the gap far below which had once been a highway. "We've lost. May as well lie down and die."

"Don't say that," said Marc. "We just have to find a way across."

"And how we going to do that, fly?"

"We climb down, find a way to ford that water, and back up the other bank. It's not impossible."

"Well, I'm glad your imagination for fantastical scenarios hasn't dimmed. And how, pray tell, are we going to get the bikes down?"

“We’d leave them here, of course, the suitcase, too. You’ll just have to pick your best, most utilitarian clothes and put them on, as many as you can wear and still feel confident you can swim in them.”

“And climb up a cliff after, apparently, while we’re sopping wet again. Damn it, Marc, I don’t want to do this.”

“You’re tough, Jain, and we don’t have a choice.”

“I’d literally murder someone for a coffee.”

“I’m the only one here, so maybe try to quell your murderous rage for a little while.”

“Oh, I’m trying, don’t you worry about that.”

Marc unzipped the suitcase, started putting on some old camouflage patterned shorts. Jain pointed at them, and said, “I’m not surprised those things will survive the apocalypse, they’ve been through everything else.”

“Get dressed, will you? Thick, durable fabrics but not too heavy when wet. You’ve got jean shorts there, and maybe this top and a jumper?” He held up the items in turn.

“I can dress myself, thank you very much.”

When they were both done putting on their chosen items, Jain picked up a small box. “I can’t leave this behind,” she said, opening it. Inside was a fine silver necklace with a small pendant of beaten silver, shaped like a heart with a small ruby set in the middle. “You gave me this for my birthday.”

Marc smiled. “I know, let me put it on you.”

She handed it to him. He looped the metal around her neck.

“A symbol of my love for you, of our bond,” he said.

She touched it gently, looking reassured by it.

***

I am Godrisaur.

I am no one's slave, no one's property. I am not one to have a collar of metal placed around my neck, a symbol of ownership and control. I am not chattel to be bought and sold, led to market by some infernal device born of humanity's cowardly cunning. They are weak and have to resort to such base treacheries.

I reach up with my clawed hands, tearing at the ring of superconducting alloy they seek to hogtie me with. It is strong and resistant to even my mighty power. I distort its shape but do not snap it. This seems to aggravate the energies running through it, sizzling through my thoughts in circles like the death spirals of the remaining helicopters I knock from the sky in my blind rage.

The fake suns of their spotlights fade, leaving their afterimages burned on my sight for a time. But after a while these go, too, and all that's left is you, the Anathema, shining in the distance like the baleful star you are, the eye of God, peering in from another dimension. But you are disappearing once more, blinking shut as you make your swift escape across the horizon, ducking into cover behind a continent.

I glare at this continent, a flat, expansive island, with only minor mountainous ripples across its surface. The coast closest to me has been smashed into muddy paste, but there is some green remaining further inland which eventually gives way beyond that to a vast barren desert of rocky red dirt and desolate yellow sands.

It is my enemy, the next hurdle, a bulwark standing between me and my destiny.

Driven mad by the flight of my prey and the coruscating energies of the collar around my neck, I step forward, towards land, towards the horizon over which the sun flees, even as my mind spins in confusion.

***

Marc's thoughts were going a million miles an hour, cogs turning furiously, trying to figure a way across this expanse of water. They'd made it down the cliff, scrambling through scrub which tore at their clothes. It had been no easy feat for Marc to climb down holding his laptop in one hand, but he was damned if he'd leave it behind.

"This necklace really gives me the energy to continue," said Jain beside him.

"Can you shut up for a second, I'm thinking," he said.

"Well, that certainly takes the romance out of it."

"I don't have time for sentiment right now. I have to get us to the other side."

The water before them was no placid pool. It was a turbulent, chaotic mass, and while it flowed past fast, this movement was not uniform, with different sections going in different directions, as if the tsunami couldn't decide if it wanted to recede back to the sea or continue its rampage of destruction further inland.

"We can't swim across," he decided.

"Because you'll get your precious laptop wet?"

"No, because we'll fucking drown!"

"Maybe we can make a raft."

"We've got no rope."

"Float across on a big log, then?" suggested Jain, starting to get panicky.

"Are you kidding?" Marc snapped. "We'd be at the mercy of the currents, dashed against these rocks."

"Well, what do we do? We're down low now. If another tidal wave comes, we're right in its path."

Marc was about to open his mouth to say there weren't any more waves coming when another vision crossed his sight, overlaid with the swirling water before him, the patterns there almost suggestive of eddies of unfolding time and fate. He saw a miniature version of

Godrisaur surging through the waves, making its way to the other side, the bank there looking like the coast of Australia. As it strove forward, it shoved water before it, the waves rippling out to strike that miniature coastline, already devastated by previous disasters, now further torn apart by successive strikes.

"Yeah, more water is coming. We have to think of something," said Marc. His mind burred with activity, running hot and loud, with the sound of waves in his eardrums. It took him a moment to realize the noise wasn't coming from the furious workings of his brain, but was something external.

It was a motor chugging away.

"Marc, look, we're saved!" said Jain, tugging at his sleeve and jumping up and down. Around the corner of the cliff came a boat. It was a white fishing boat, bigger than a dinghy, perhaps six meters long, with an outboard motor and a canopy overhead. On the side the name of the boat—*Holey Moley*—was written in blue cursive letters. A man with a grey beard, ruddy skin, and a cheesy fake captain's hat stood at the silver steering wheel, a sharp-faced dog sitting erect on the seat beside him.

"Ahoy there!" cried Marc, immediately regretting it and feeling stupid. But then the man on the boat saw them and returned the greeting with a hearty wave.

"Got yourself in a bit of a spot, have you?" he shouted. "Not too bright."

I'm not the one with the dumb hat, Marc thought, though with instant regret that he was judging someone who might help them.

The boat fought against the rippling currents, the man deftly piloting it against the conflicting swirls of eddying water to bring it close to the slither of bank on which Marc and Jain stood at the base of the cliff. The dog jumped up on the boat's edge and started barking, which made the pair step back in fright and press themselves against the rocks behind.

"Oh, don't mind Mister Cloverfield here. He's a bit aggressive towards strangers," said the man.

"That's an odd name for a dog," said Marc, thinking he was making small talk. The sour look the man gave him and the jab in the ribs from Jain persuaded him otherwise.

"Nice to meet you, too," said the man sarcastically.

"Oh, I'm sorry. Hello, I'm Marc with a C, and this is my partner Jain, which isn't spelled how you would expect."

"I'm Tom with a T, and it's spelled exactly how you'd expect."

"Funny," said Jain.

"Then why didn't you laugh?" said Tom, completely deadpan. There was a long pause where he stared at them, the boat's engine rumbling, accompanied by the low ominous growling of Mister Cloverfield.

Okay, this guy's weird, thought Marc.

"We're trying to get to the other bank over there, do you think you could help us out?" he asked to break the tension and get straight to the point. It felt like the more they delayed and made small talk the greater the chance Tom would get sick of them and drive off.

"Yeah, could do. What do you have in trade?" said Tom.

"Trade?" asked Jain. "You want us to pay you? It's a fifty meter ride and you're already here."

"I ain't ferrying people around for nothing. Is that a laptop you've got there?"

"I'm not giving you my laptop," said Marc, tucking it into his jacket defensively.

"Then what else you got? Boat fuel is pretty costly, you know, and I'm wasting it idling here."

Marc noticed Tom was very careful to keep his boat far enough away they couldn't jump onto it.

What's this guy's deal? Doesn't he want to help people?

"I think we've all got bigger concerns than the cost of fuel, mate," said Jain.

Tom leaned overboard and spat in the water. "You do. I'm fine."

"You know this is the end of civilization, don't you?" Marc asked.

"This? Not bloomin' likely. How long you lived in the valley? It floods every few years."

"Not from a tsunami it doesn't."

"Water's water. Speaking of, you want to cross, I need some payment."

Marc swept a hand down his clothing. "All we've got is what we're standing in."

"No cash?"

"What are you going to do with cash?" asked Jain, getting annoyed.

"Spend it."

Not anytime soon, thought Marc.

"We don't have any cash," he said.

Tom scratched his chin thoughtfully. "Jewelry, then."

Jain flinched, clutching at her neck as if Tom had reached out with an impossibly long arm and tried to snatch her necklace away.

"Ah," said Tom, propping a foot up on the side of his boat and leaning on his knee. "I see we've got some sparkle sparkle after all."

Jain turned to Marc. "I'm not giving him my fucking necklace," she said, shaking her head, her whole body following suit like a shiver of rage running down her spine.

Marc put a hand on her shoulder. "No, I don't want you to either, but—"

"But the ferryman must be paid!" said Tom, jabbing a finger at the sky as if expounding some fine philosophical point. Mister Cloverfield punctuated its owner's sentence with a single menacing bark, drool hanging from its pink mouth filled with yellowing teeth.

"Give him your fucking laptop if you want to give him something so bad," hissed Jain between her teeth.

"That's my book on there," said Marc.

"Your book isn't on there, it's in here," said Jain, tapping his head with a finger.

I much prefer when the monster gets out of my head and onto the page, thank you very much, Marc thought but didn't say.

"It's just a memory, you can recreate it," said Jain. There was a pleading tone in her voice. She wasn't making an argument for giving up the laptop as much as it being easier to give up than her necklace.

"The necklace is just a memory, too. We can buy a new one," said Marc, moving to hug her. She stepped back, anger twisting her face.

"And when and how exactly will we get back to that silversmith in Bali if this is the end of the world?"

"You could say the same about my computer."

"It's called pen and paper, Marc. Write books like your damned dead heroes did!"

"But what about what I've already got saved, the effort I've already invested? All that will be lost."

"Think about what you have already invested in me and what you'll lose if you force me to give this up," said Jain. Her hand was grasping the love heart pendant in a white knuckled fist. "If there's no electricity you can't even use that thing. Come on, Marc, it's just an old laptop. What is that versus our lives?"

"You've talked me out of the laptop good and proper, haven't you?" said Tom, going back to stand by his steering wheel. He cranked up the engine and began to turn away. "Look, it's either give up the bling, or you can stay on that bank to rot."

Distracted, Jain's hand loosened on the pendant. Marc could see the conflicting thoughts in her mind dancing back and forth as her eyes jumped from the boat to the far bank and back.

Taking advantage of her distraction, Marc stepped in, snatched the necklace from her neck, breaking the fine silver chain with a sharp tug.

"Ouch! What the fuck, Marc?" said Jain, jumping back and lifting a defensive hand. That hand quickly flew to her bare neck and she gasped in shock. "You took it. I can't believe you did that."

Marc held the necklace up like a talisman used to summon a messenger of the Gods, and it brought Tom and his boat chugging up to the embankment. Mister Cloverfield barked furiously, snapping his jaws so hard the teeth clicked loudly. Jumping aboard, Marc gave the dog a push with his shoe to fend it off and drive it back, clearing the way for Jain to follow him up over the rail. He turned to offer her a hand up, but she ignored it and clambered on board further along.

"Don't kick my fucking dog or I'll throw you over the side," said Tom, extending a hand, not to shake, but palm up, expecting immediate payment.

Marc smacked the necklace down hard into the open palm. "Tell your little monster not to bite or you're both going in the fucking drink, you got it, mate?"

Tom must have caught a hint of the madness in Marc's eyes, because he backed off and busied himself with piloting the boat.

"You don't want to see the monster I got inside me, mate," muttered Marc, taking a seat at the front of the boat. He looked across at Jain, sitting opposite, and the anger he felt was paled by the fury he saw burning in her eyes.

15

All is darkness and I am in a purgatory worse than any hell. Agony would be preferable to this nothingness I feel, my brain numbed by the swirling energies coursing around my neck. I cannot think straight. This electromagnetic collar has decapitated me more effectively than any blow by the sword of a God. Unlike a mundane wound, no blood flows from the stump of my neck. There is no outward sign that I am destroyed and defeated. I would welcome such a thing, because then at least my destiny would be sealed, the matter decided.

But no, I am in limbo, like a criminal hung from his feet, all the blood rushing to their head so they cannot even ponder their own fate. I have no thoughts; even these words tumble out of my ears like melted wax, not processed, not remembered, but immediately lost to the cosmos as soon as they are conjured. I am left with nothing but my emotions, driven not by reason but by the shattered feelings of a Demi-God denied.

I am sad and confused, a lost child. I am angry, enraged by my predicament and my abandonment. This world birthed me and then left me at the mercy of these festering insects which have swarmed across my skin, making it crawl. They are not worthy. Humanity is not an idol to be worshipped, not a noble foe like the sun. It is a menace to be removed, scoured from this Earth.

And I am the architect of that fortune, the destruction of mankind well-deserved. I will not be bound like a prize hog, placed upon the spit for the wicked demons to devour. I am not the lesser being, but the greater.

I must be free! I will not wear your ring of lead and other base metals. I am worth more than the silver sheen of this trinket. I am gold. I am lava. I am molten fire.

Driven mad with rage, I claw at the collar around my neck. Even my colossal strength is impotent against it, even with all my anger fueling me as I tug at it. In my fury, all I do is tear my own skin, lava flowing down my neck and over the collar.

It sizzles as I cry. My magma tears fall on the collar as well, adding to the effect which has now begun. I can smell the burning of metal, and, twisting my head at a hard angle, I can see my boiling volcano blood is doing the collar a mischief. It is melting those metals; they cannot stand the terrific temperatures of the viscous lava coating it.

With a roar to awaken the heavens and shake the stars in the night sky, I reach up with both my clawed hands, wrap them around the distorted, softening metal collar. With a tug filled with all the desperate rage at my enslavement, I pull.

There is a moment of give. Then the collar goes taut, resists—and snaps.

It falls from my neck, from my hands, no longer a circle but a broken, mangled ring. It does not encapsulate me any longer. It is not my infinite destiny, just a single fleeting moment of my life, now passed. The length of hot metal drops into the ocean, where it boils the water as it sinks into the depths, never to trouble me again as I step over it, leaving it behind me forever.

***

"My wife will love this," said Tom, pocketing the necklace and placing both hands on the steering wheel. Marc seethed in his thoughts.

God, rub it in why don't you?

"Your wife is lucky to have such a romantic man to give her jewelry," said Jain. Her snarky tone was lost on Tom, who beamed as if it was an unironic compliment.

"That she is. Very lucky to have me," said Tom as he revved the engine and steered the boat into the confusing swirl of currents. "I'm a provider, I am. Lots of blokes would be sitting at home right now. But I'm out here, earning us a crust when most would be cowering away."

"You're a real entrepreneur," said Marc, matching Jain's tone, which she didn't take lightly to, giving him a death stare which warned him to stay out of her baiting.

Clearly it's the only thing giving her any comfort, he thought, dropping his head.

Mister Cloverfield must have taken this as a sign of weakness as he barked once, loud and sharp. It was a shock to the ears and hit Marc like a slap. He only had a split second to look up as the dog bounded the few meters down the length of the boat.

"What the fuck?" said Marc as the dog leapt at him. Without thinking he extended his arms to fend the dog off. There was a moment of pure terror where he was sure the dog was going to bite his arm, gouge a big gory chunk out of the flesh which would surely get infected. He got a flash of this projected future timeline and his chances didn't look good without access to medical help. A terrible death by rabies or tetanus awaited him.

But the dog didn't go for his arms, it went for his face, snapping its slavering jaws. Marc's outstretched arms slipped underneath its belly, and, on pure instinct, he dropped his head and pushed up with his hands.

Mister Cloverfield flew overhead, the dog aided in its flight by a quick, unconscious shove by Marc, disappearing over the side of the boat. It was all over in a moment, punctuated by a splash and a shout of surprised alarm from Tom.

"Boy!" said the man, abandoning the steering wheel and rushing forward. He gripped the boat's side and peered into the drink, his face one of childlike terror. Marc stood up and turned, took a cautious step back from

Tom, and was joined by Jain, who rushed across. They stared into the choppy currents, but there was no sign of the dog in the muddy brown water.

It was hard to even guess where the canine had gone in, a problem exacerbated by the unattended steering wheel, which rotated as the boat was manhandled violently by the churning floodwater. They were drifting off-station and all the water looked the same, a violent maelstrom of swirling eddies shifting and morphing each second. Tom grabbed a red life preserver ring but couldn't decide where to throw the thing, so he tossed it down on the deck in frustration.

"You've bloody killed him, you fucking bastard!" he spat, his terror turning to blind rage the second he realized the dog wasn't going to resurface, that there was no hope of saving the mutt.

Marc and Jain backed off a step or two, but the enraged boatman pounced forward, attacking with the same mindless viciousness of his dog, his face a savage mask of grief and fury. There was nowhere to run and they were only saved from the wild haymaker punch Tom threw by the lurch of the boat as the engine revved. He stumbled, bent half over, and Marc kneed him in the face.

Tom cursed but came on like a rugby player attempting a tackle. Behind him the steering wheel stopped at the far lock in one direction, turning the boat in a tight circle which knocked the charging man off balance. Marc and Jain nearly went overboard as they jumped aside to avoid him, and Tom fell heavily against the bow of the boat. He growled like a feral beast and spat a string of indecipherable invective, his face a horrifying crimson mask.

Looking around for a weapon, he grabbed a piece of anchor chain and swung it at Marc and Jain as they retreated, but was foiled as it was attached to the front of the boat and couldn't reach. He dropped it with a snarl of frustration, looking around for an alternative. An idea dawning on his face, he reached into a compartment, produced a sheathed fishing knife. As he pulled it from the khaki cloth scabbard a sparkle of triumph flashed across his face, mirrored in the sheen of the blade in the light of the setting sun. The white boat was splashed red, the blood color of fading light making Tom look like a terrible demon from the depths of hell as he advanced.

"Don't fucking kill us over a damned dog," said Marc, trying to make it sound enough like an order that Tom would second guess himself and hesitate. It didn't work, Tom taking a step forward menacingly.

"This is murder!" shrieked Jain, her voice so shrill and piercing it did actually give Tom pause for a moment. The man grimaced and lunged at them, mad with grief, a strangled cry on his lips.

He went for Jain first, through cowardice—she being much smaller than him—or perhaps wishing Marc to suffer the same fate he had, to witness the death of a loved one. Either way, Marc was thankful as it gave him time to grab for an object he'd just caught sight of.

It was a short wooden club, the type a fisherman uses to brain a caught fish, put it out of its misery. As Tom drove his stabbing knife at Jain, driving her back in terror, Marc put the club to its intended use, smacking Tom hard across the skull with all his strength. There was an audible crack and Tom fell like a dropped sack of shit into the bottom of the boat, the knife skittering on the deck.

Jain ran back and gave him a solid kick around the head with a meaty sound, making sure he stayed down. Marc, his blood up, went a step further, scooping up the fallen knife and plunging it into Tom's back. There was a gurgle of frothy blood on the man's lips; he'd been stabbed through the lung.

Marc stepped back in horror at what he had done, his eyes fixed on the handle of the knife standing erect from Tom's back.

"Good bloody riddance, you opportunist piece of shit," said Jain, spitting on Tom. She reached down, fished through his pocket, and retrieved her necklace. The chain was broken so she didn't put it on, but placed it in her own pocket.

Tom groaned, then coughed violently, rolling over and reaching for Jain's ankle. She screamed and jumped back. Marc reflexively swung the club down, striking Tom in the eye socket. The bone gave way and the vicious blow minced his eye to jelly. The other eye shot open in mortal terror and he began to convulse.

Jain whimpered and Marc stared in horror as the man floundered like a drowning fish in the bottom of the boat.

"Oh God, Marc, make it stop," said Jain, burying her face in her folded arms. Marc hefted the club one last time and brought it down in a sharp blow to Tom's temple, putting him out of his misery once and for all.

***

With the collar gone the pain of loss returns—the Anathema has abandoned me. It is a physical pain. I feel it jabbing into my brain now the spinning sensation has ceased. The needle of my internal compass is sharp and hard, a sword pointing both outward and inward, impaling my mind and tormenting me with thoughts of the road ahead and the road traveled. Though it is strange for a monster as large and mighty as I to admit, I feel sorry for myself, as if my entire creation is nothing but a lie, that I am doomed to return to the bottom of the ocean empty handed.

I open my mouth and let out a roar. Sunlight shines forth from my throat like an impossibly bright spotlight, tracing its beam across the night sky. This reminds me I have been victorious before, and I gain heart. There were once two suns which revolved around this Earth, now only one, the other residing in my belly, the pair separated.

Alone, they are weak and easy to destroy.

Just like you.

16

Marc and Jain didn't speak, and Marc felt far away from her, an impossible barrier between them. He stepped up to the steering wheel, wobbly and uncertain on his feet as the boat careened around in a circle, the engine revving. Grabbing the wheel, he had to pull hard to bring the boat under control, the rudder fighting him. Only reluctantly did the currents swirling around the boat loosen their grip as he dragged the wheel over hard, using his bodyweight to pull them out of their spinning pattern amidst the choppy floodwaters.

They shot along a line parallel with the two banks, far too fast, and Marc dragged back on the throttle, careful not to do so too swiftly or all the way down, fearful of the engine cutting out and stranding them. He had to work the wheel deftly with the other hand as they slowed to dodge large pieces of debris bobbing on the waves and tangled wreckage jutting up out of the water.

It was only at this point did he notice there were bodies floating by, grisly masses of flotsam and jetsam among the logs and shattered building materials. Marc grimaced.

I killed a man.

The thought seemed distant, like the setting sun, ready to hide behind the wall of his subconscious, there to fester but at least out of sight. He couldn't confront the truth of it, not directly, so he began the process of dissembling, his mind talking to itself back and forth.

I had to do it. He was going to hurt us.

Damn that dog. What sort of name is Mister Cloverfield anyway?

It's just one more person dead. What does that matter in all this destruction?

One life lost versus two saved—my own and Jain's—it's simple math.

Marc looked across at Jain. She was staring at the dead body. Marc frowned and steered them towards the far bank.

***

One life is nothing to me. My death toll is measured in the millions. I devastate whole continents, ravage entire civilizations and wipe them from the face of the Earth.

I am Godrisaur.

I am terror manifest, death incarnate.

You are nothing to me.

***

Marc pushed the throttle forward at the last second and rammed the boat hard up against the bank to beach it. The currents tugged at its tail but the nose was sunk deep into grassy mud and held firm.

"Let's go," he said, moving to jump off.

"Wait, he could have some useful stuff," said Jain, snapping out of her reverie and looking at Marc, or through him. There was a glassy quality to her eyes and she looked more afraid than ever.

Perhaps the reality of the life or death predicament we're in has finally hit home, thought Marc.

He pointed. "Okay, I think those benches there lift up. Check inside. I'll go see what else was in that compartment he got…"

Marc trailed off.

The compartment Tom got the knife from.

He shuddered, but forced himself to look in the little hatch. There was basic fishing gear in a plastic box, a hand line, some sinkers and hooks, some dried bait. He took it.

"There's some bottled water," said Jain, "and a bag of beef jerky."

Marc made a face. "Meat…ugh."

"You might not have the luxury of being a vegetarian anymore. And if you won't eat it, I will."

Mark held up his find. "I might have to get used to fish."

"There's also a bottle of booze. It's vodka." Jain mirrored the look Marc had for the meat. They were both years sober.

"We should take it," said Marc.

"What?"

"I don't think either of us should start drinking again. And the end of the world is no excuse. It'll add disaster upon disaster. But it could be useful, medically speaking. What if one of us is hurt and we need to disinfect the wound?"

"Marc, I was a nurse for years. Vodka doesn't have a high enough concentration to disinfect a cut."

"Well, maybe my parents might need a stiff drink. We don't know what they've been through."

"I'm not carrying it."

"I will. Besides, we might need it for barter. That bottle is money now."

"There's a rough hessian sack here."

"Okay, give it to me and I'll carry everything." He took the items, loaded them in the sack, and went to disembark.

"What about the knife?" said Jain. "It could be a useful tool in a survival situation." She was staring morbidly at the body again.

Marc didn't look back as he jumped down onto the bank. "I'm not touching that fucking thing."

***

They climbed up the cliff facing the ravine, thankfully less steep than the one they had descended and covered in scrubby tufts of yellowed grass they could use as handholds. Marc wanted to say something, to talk about what had happened, not so much the murder, but the incident with the necklace, the way he'd snatched it from her, traded it away. He was glad Jain had it back, though he was less than pleased with how the whole thing had gone down.

For her part, Jain was keeping quiet, either in shock as a result of the murder, or at what she perceived as a betrayal of their love. Perhaps it was both. Killing Tom, while allowing them to retrieve the necklace, didn't exactly undo the hurt. But he'd done it for her all the same, to protect her and so they didn't have to go through this awful mess without the other by their side.

It was only then Marc realized he himself could have died. He'd only been thinking about saving Jain, but, instinctually at least, he'd protected himself as well, first against Mister Cloverfield, then against Tom.

Breathing hard from the exertion of climbing brought Marc back to the moment. He was glad to be alive. Jain was a little behind, and reaching the top of the cliff first, Marc turned and looked at her. There wasn't much light, what was left of the moon hidden behind ominous cloud. But in gloom he could see the strain in her face, the toll the crossing had cost her, just as it had cost him.

They were both different people now, having each left a previous version of themselves on the other bank. Like the missing bridge that had been swept away by the unstoppable tsunami, there was little connecting these two worlds, these two people, the past and present Marc. Perhaps Jain felt similarly split in two, separated from a part of herself so suddenly, the innocent person she had been before confronted with death. Of course, in all her years in the hospital she would have seen death many times, though Marc was sure it wasn't the same as participating in a murder. Even committed in self-defense, killing left a scar. Marc inspected that scar inside himself, saw it was raw and would take a long time to heal, but he didn't have time for it now, and he wondered if there would ever be time to come to terms with it.

Will the ghost of Tom haunt me in my dreams? What's one more death amidst all this destruction?

He crested the cliff. Far below, the river of bodies and debris flowed by, heard but unseen in the dense gloom. The sound of the rushing water gave those corpses a voice, and it was a roar like a monster, a scream like a banshee.

No wonder Jain was silent as she reached the top.

All this must be weighing on her as much as it does on me, thought Marc, extending a hand to help her up the last step, which she ignored. Panting, she put her hands on her hips, turned back towards the horizon, back towards the direction of the ocean, as if to see how far they had come.

Maybe she's pleased, proud of herself for overcoming such a difficult obstacle.

"Why do we get to live when all those others perished?" she asked, and Marc realized he'd guessed wrong. Instead, she was suffering from survivor's guilt.

"Luck combined with action, I suppose," he said, the only answer he could come up with.

"We don't deserve it."

"You have to try to save yourself, everyone does. It just worked out for us. There's no right or wrong in it, it's just what happened."

"Good people died."

And we're not good people, we're murderers, or, at least, I am, Marc thought.

"There's still hope," he said.

She ignored this, pointed towards the east. "What's that light? It can't be dawn already. The sun only just went down."

There was a large beam of illumination expanding like a wide fan up into the night sky from a point just over the horizon.

"A searchlight?" suggested Marc.

Jain shook her head. "Looks too big for that, but maybe the Navy is out there with some high-tech stuff, helping people."

The light flickered off for a few moments, then back on. This repeated several times at irregular intervals.

"Is it a lighthouse?" asked Marc.

"World's most ridiculously bright lighthouse, plus there's no standard timing. And it's not like the beam is sweeping around in a circle. It's all over the shop."

The light flashed back and forth like a giant waving a sword as it straddled the horizon. Marc had a sinking feeling in his guts. A spike of panic hit his brain as the beam swept inland towards them. "Fuck, it seems to be coming this way. Do we hide?"

"From what? If it's a rescue light we want them to see us," said Jain. She started jumping up and down on the spot, waving her arms and shouting, "Hey, over here!"

"No," said Marc, realizing finally what the light was. "Watch out! Get the fuck down!" He grabbed at her, but she resisted. She went to say something, but was cut off as the beam sliced by overhead.

It was impossibly fat, wider than the torrent of water flowing between the cliffs, and the brightness forced their eyes shut. Even so, it left searing afterimages on Marc's sight and lit up his eyelids a bright pink.

Jain dropped down to the ground and Marc threw himself across her as a series of popping bangs sounded overhead, hurting their ears with the overpressure. A rain of sharp splinters immediately followed. Jain tensed beneath him, and he was sure she was screaming by the way her chest was flexing, but he couldn't hear anything over a whooshing sound which filled his ears. He opened his eyes, and through the flashing, colorful stars, fading each moment, he saw that the trees along the edge of the cliff were on fire.

Or, at least, what was left of them.

The beam had sliced through the trees like a hot knife, heating them so quickly their trunks had exploded, peppering the area with wooden shrapnel. Their shattered remains burned with a fierce intensity, emitting a wail which rose and fell on the wind. The flames twisted and turned as if they were alive. They seemed to bend towards Jain and Marc like fiery ghosts inspecting their prey closely before deciding whether to consume them.

"Fuck, fuck, fuck," said Jain, choking on the sudden ash which swirled around them.

"What is it?" asked Marc, and felt stupid for asking. Their situation warranted at least one fuck, but he immediately saw she was referring to something in particular.

A large, sharp fragment of wood had impaled the meat of her left thigh. Dark blood oozed from the wound.

"Oh, no, Jain, fuck!" said Marc. "You're the nurse, what do I do?"

She began whimpering in pain, her face an ugly grimace of despair, puffed up and red.

"Should I leave it in or pull it out?" he asked. When she didn't answer, he grabbed the piece of wood jutting out of her and gave it a tug to test its purchase. She screamed and hit him in the chest with a fist.

"You fucking asshole, you're meant to leave it in," she said. Her tears left smears through the ash falling on her face.

"Look, help isn't coming, Jain, we still have to walk out of here." He looked around at the burning forest, aware time was pressing. "I can't even bind up the wound with this hunk of wood in the way."

"I could bleed out."

Marc emptied the hessian sack. "I'll make a tourniquet with this."

She nodded weakly.

Not giving her time to object, Marc wrapped his hand in the sack to get a grip on the piece of wood, slick with her blood, said, "Okay, on the count of three," and ripped the splinter out without ever starting the count.

She screamed. The terrible, shocking agony in her voice broke his heart, but he tried to ignore it as he unwound the sack from his hand.

"Alcohol first," said Jain, lying back flat but jabbing a finger at her leg.

"I thought you said it wasn't strong enough to disinfect?"

"Better than bloody nothing, isn't it?"

Marc shrugged and cracked the top off the vodka. He gave the wound a wash with the stuff, careful to ward off any falling embers. Jain hissed at the stinging.

"Now give me the bottle," she said, grasping blindly towards him with a hand.

"I'm not letting you drink this."

She propped herself up on an elbow. "You want me to walk, don't you? Or, at least, hobble along beside you."

"I'll carry you."

Jain gave him a dubious look, but didn't challenge him. Instead she said, "I need to numb the pain."

"You're tough," he said and threw the bottle over the cliff. She watched it arc away with wide, disbelieving eyes, as if he'd tossed one of her family members off the edge. Those eyes reflected the burning flames of the forest as they turned on Marc.

17

Jain seethed as Marc doused the hessian sack in water and tied it as tightly as he could around the wound. It was stained with oozing blood immediately, but seemed to staunch the flow.

"Okay, on your feet," he said. "We can't stay here."

With a long string of invective from both of them, they got her on her feet. He turned his back to her, held his arms behind himself to carry her.

"I'll just jump up, will I?" she said, and shoved him aside. She took a few defiant steps before she got shaky, nearly toppling over into a burning shrub. Leaning on a rock, she pulled her hand away with a start. "Ouch, that's hot."

Marc went over to her and she leaned against him. The heat from the conflagration around them was starting to suck away the oxygen and even Marc felt a bit unsteady on his feet. Without further preamble, he bent down, threw her over his shoulder and lifted her in a fireman's carry.

"Lucky I've been working out so much lately," he said.

"And what's that supposed to mean?"

"That you're light as a feather."

"Exactly."

Marc was already moving, dodging between the trees, trying to stay clear of the worst blazes. There were fallen logs to avoid, some on fire, others simply too large to cross while carrying Jain. He focused on taking one step at a time, his shoes sifting through the ash and splinters covering the ground. His feet were starting to get hot.

"I think the soles of my shoes are melting," he said, coughing around the words. The smoke was getting intense. Jain didn't respond, which worried him. He looked around, desperate for any respite from the heat and lack of air, and saw a gully. It was a firebreak, a ditch dug to prevent fires spreading. He put Jain down on the edge of it. She mumbled something weakly. Clambering down into the gully, he eased her back onto his shoulders. He had to hunch down low to stay out of the thickening smoke, but Jain was weighing him down anyway. His strength was quickly starting to be sapped away.

He couldn't keep this up for much longer.

***

Reaching the continental shelf, I step up and out of the deep water. Rising higher than the tallest buildings, my head scrapes the clouds of the overcast sky. The ocean cascades off my back like a roaring waterfall.

I inspect the devastation wrought by the waves of displaced water. At first I am happy; the bite taken from the coast is hundreds of kilometers long, leaving a terrible gouge in the side of the continent. It is a collapsed crater, the site of some awful explosion beyond the imagination of men.

But I'm disappointed all the same. The width of the wound does not match its length, and while water still scours the inland countryside, it has not reached as far I would have hoped. This destruction was meant to herald my arrival, to be a taste of the things to come. To know that some mercy was shown by my elemental wrath fills me with a quaking rage which only destruction will quench.

My horror and humiliation is complete when I witness that there are still skyscrapers standing, the buildings lined up a few dozen kilometers from the coast, a demarcation of the farthest limit of the massive waves' reach. These structures are like the arms of my enemies raised in a defiant salute.

I cannot suffer this. My roar of anger rocks the ocean and spreads through the bedrock of the seabed, sending ripples into the continent as I stride forward to wreak my vengeance upon the cities of man.

***

"What the hell was that?" hissed Marc, not expecting and not getting an answer from Jain. The ground beneath his feet shook violently, the walls of the gulley swaying so significantly he expected they would collapse at any moment, crushing them to death. Many trees, half burned through, did indeed tumble, showering them in sparks and splinters. Ash fell in such thickness it was as if a truckload of the stuff had been dumped on them at once. Marc was forced to quickly lower Jain to the ground. He threw himself across her to shield her and cover her wound the best he could.

She mumbled something, drowsy with blood loss. Marc felt her blood running down his back from where he'd carried her, could see it on his arm. He inspected the tourniquet by the light of the burning trees. It was completely soaked through.

"Damn it, we're not dying here," he said, his fingers slick with blood as he tugged hard to tighten the hessian sack.

***

Death comes with every dread footfall of my monstrous bulk, with every swipe of my long tail. The skyscrapers cannot resist the crushing embrace of my powerful arms. Men and women flee like ants before me and die just as easily as the buildings come down, smothered in huge twisted piles of ruined concrete, glass, and steel. These are their gravestones, the only markers to commemorate their meaningless lives.

I stride across their final resting place without reverence, without pause. There is no one to oppose me, no cunning stratagem by humanity's militaries left to deploy against me. Now there is only destruction, my purpose made manifest.

The balance of the world is undone, the scales tipped. There can be no life where I walk.

Death is your only companion now.

***

"Please, Jain, get up," begged Marc. "You're my life companion. You're everything to me. Without you, life isn't worth living. Please, get up."

He shook her shoulder until she stirred.

"What is it?" she murmured, looking around with bleary eyes which were only bloodshot slits in a blackened face. "It's not time to go to work yet, is it?"

"Wake up! I don't have time for any nonsense."

"Is the house on fire?" she asked, perking up a little.

Marc rolled his eyes. "Yes, the house is on fire, we need to get out."

To his utter shock, she pushed herself up with surprising agility, and, ignoring the wound in her leg, began to run down the gulley.

"Fuck, that's adrenaline for you," he said, feeling his own fear spike the chemical in his bloodstream as he glanced around at the inferno closing in. Then he realized he'd lost sight of Jain in the smoke and pure terror shot through him, giving him all the speed he needed to bolt after her.

He found her in a clearing of black asphalt, a turning bay before a gate outside a house. The pain seemed to have caught up with her a bit as she was hobbling now, favoring her good leg, slowing but not stopping. For a moment Marc considered running up to the house and asking for help. But he quickly dismissed the idea; if anyone was up there they'd have their own problems.

More than likely they'd probably try to blow our heads off if they see a pair of soot-covered lunatics rushing their house, smeared with blood.

Still, he had his eye out for anything they could use to their advantage. The road leading past the house was helpful. He actually knew where they were and could follow that road all the way to his parents' house. But Jain's adrenaline would wear off soon and they'd be back in a similar predicament as before, though with the one advantage that the road provided a natural corridor through the burning bush, sparing them the worst of the heat and saving them from a fiery death.

The smoke was still a problem and the air clogged with ash. He took a water bottle from his pocket. Tearing a strip of cloth from the bottom of his shirt, he doused it in the water and wrapped it around his nose and mouth. Then he ran up to something useful he'd seen a moment earlier, a wheelbarrow. He tried to call out to Jain to stop, but she couldn't hear him, and it was probably for the best; let her get as far as she can on her own.

He took the wheelbarrow by the handles and rushed after her, pushing it before him.

"Here, get in," he said. He had to yell to be heard above the loud crackling of burning trees all around. She didn't acknowledge him or turn, so he rammed the wheelbarrow up her backside. She tumbled into its tray and he took the sudden load as gracefully as he could on the trot, wobbling and swerving for a while before correcting and finding balance. This wasn't easy as Jain squirmed around, trying to turn around and curse him out. He ignored her and ran down the road, the burning trees rising up either side like pillars to the gates of hell.

***

I bring hell to Earth. I open my mouth and let loose the energy of a miniature sun. I incinerate all which isn't crushed beneath my mass.

In my wake there are no tears, for none survive. All is a flattened wasteland, with only flame and smoke rising above the desolate plains.

18

The asphalt road was hot, superheated by the furious forest fire all around. Both these factors, not to mention Jain's state, spurred Marc on to greater speeds, desperate to get clear of the wooded area. His footfalls were tacky, sticking with each step, the soles of his shoes melting. His feet were burning, but nothing could be done about this. There was nowhere to go but forward, through the fire and hopefully out the other side. It helped that the winding road was heading slightly downhill, which lightened the load. Jain had slumped back and was drifting in and out of consciousness, but Marc was fading fast himself, the air hot and hard to breathe. Every now and then he had to stop and bend low to get at some oxygen free of smoke.

It was hard to see, but he'd driven this road many times on the way to visit his folks.

Not long now, he thought, picturing the place on the road where the tree-line ended, giving way to a stretch where there was a bare cliff rising up to one side of the road and sloping down on the other. He pushed through the pain—each slap of his feet on the searing hot asphalt was torture—and kept his eyes fixed on Jain, hoping she was getting enough oxygen.

"The best thing you can do for her is get her clear," he said, ignoring his back, which was screaming at him to stop and drop the load. It was hard to see much beyond their little island of the wheelbarrow, but the glow of the fire beyond the smoke gave him a guide, kept him in the narrow corridor where they wouldn't be instantly consumed by the flames.

When he finally reached the edge of the woods he could hardly believe it. Clear night air smacked him in the face so hard he skidded to a halt as if he'd run into a wall. He stumbled and jackknifed the wheelbarrow, sending it, and Jain, tumbling onto the road.

"Jain!" he said, rushing forward to help her.

She was wincing and hissing, her confusion and discomfort evident. There were some cuts and scrapes up her arms where she'd landed, and a little gash on her forehead. A bead of blood formed and trickled down into her eye.

"Ugh, what the fuck?" she said, wiping her eye, trying to clear it and only succeeding in smudging a red smear through the soot on her face.

"Hold on a second," he said, pulling out the last of the water. He desperately wanted a drink to wash the ash out of his dry throat, but instead he carefully used a small portion of the water to clear Jain's eye and then handed her the bottle. "Here, drink this."

She shakily took the bottle, her grip weak, and raised it to her lips. "God, I feel like I've swallowed a bag of razors," she said, sipping at the water.

"You and me both," he replied, smiling. His bright white teeth appeared suspended in his sooty face alongside his eyes like some grinning Cheshire cat in a fairy tale. The forest fire raged behind his head, making his silhouette even more sinister.

"Are we in hell?" asked Jain.

"Yes, unfortunately, but damned if we're staying long."

"My leg, it hurts." She looked at it. "Fuck, that doesn't look good."

Blood was oozing out of the bandage again. Marc ripped off his jacket, did a double take when he saw how singed it was, and removed his shirt. Putting the jacket back on with a silent prayer thanking it for protecting him from the fire so much, he tied the shirt around Jain's thigh above the wound and hessian sack. He tugged hard on it to get it super tight. She gritted her teeth against the pain, but stood it well, understanding he was trying to cut off the flow of blood.

"That's the best I can do. Let's get you back in the wheelbarrow," he said, grabbing her under the armpits and helping her to her feet. He propped her up on her good leg, took a step back, hands out, wary that she'd fall, like a delicately balanced vase. When he was certain she wasn't going over straight away, he quickly righted the wheelbarrow and guided her into the tray again. She went a lot more willingly this time, her strength totally sapped. The adrenaline had long since worn off for the both of them, but Marc didn't have the luxury of stopping. He hefted the handles of the wheelbarrow. It was only a few steps before his shoes fell to charred pieces and sloughed off his feet, taking some of the skin with it.

"That'd be bloody right, wouldn't it?" said Marc, and began to hobble the last couple of kilometers to his parents' place, cursing the name Godrisaur the whole time.

***

The world burns beneath my feet. The sky is seared with my light. If I cannot swallow a second sun, then the world will know the fury of the first, the one already in my guts. I spew its energy across the land, leveling cities and turning forests to ash with incinerating blasts of an unleashed star.

I know no resistance. No one can stand against me. I am an island of vitality in a sea of death.

***

Marc was not going to let any pain, any barrier of man nor God, stop him from reaching his destination. He reached mental and physical thresholds he didn't know existed, and then pushed through each in turn, only to find more beyond, each more mind-numbingly excruciating than the last.

But he had Jain. His love for her lifted his feet, one step at a time, and drove him on. And though this was enough to comfort him through his agonizing struggle, there was something else willing him forward as well.

You're not going to beat me, he said internally, directing the thought at Godrisaur. Somehow he knew it could hear him, that the two of them were mysteriously linked.

With each thump of his feet on the road his heart beat in sympathetic unison. It felt hot in his chest, like a miniature sun, burning with rage directed at the monster. When Marc opened his mouth to vent his furious frustration, this spark of light shone from deep inside of him. It stretched out ahead of him, guiding him home, invisible perhaps to everyone else, but enough for him to see by, to light his way.

19

Entering the village was an eerie experience. Why Marc expected the place to be in an uproar he wasn't sure. Perched on a hill at the end of the ridge, overlooking the sugarcane fields of the valley—all flooded with water now—and the mountain ranges hemming them in to the north, the village was out of town and used to being cut off in times of natural disaster. Even a storm could easily knock the power out, and, as Tom had so poignantly pointed out, the valley was used to floods.

To residents of the village this was just another blackout, another flood, isolating them in their houses with their backup stockpiles of food and water put aside for such an occasion. Without power, and with the mobile phone towers down—not that the village got reception at the best of times anyway—the people were unaware of the greater disaster unfolding beyond their little pocket of civilization.

The windows of the houses were dark. It was late and people turned in early when the power was out, the boredom and darkness driving them to their beds, hoping to hurry the return of morning when light made mundane tasks and entertaining distractions easier. The moonlight shone on the asphalt through a hole in silver clouds and glistened on the grass, moist from the dampness of the air. Marc diverted his path off the road onto these cool lawns, letting them soothe his burned and peeling feet, but found it to be even more painful, as the change of sensation awakened deadened nerves and sent shockwaves of tingling pain up his legs.

Suddenly, with only a few hundred meters to go, it all seemed too much, too far, the wheelbarrow and Jain impossibly heavy.

"Are you alright?" asked a voice. Marc swiveled his head and the question was repeated. It came from the yawning black doorway of the closest house, as if the house itself was speaking. A light kindled in that open portal and grew in intensity, and for a second, Marc was sure he was staring down the gullet of Godrisaur, the power of the sun in its guts building, ready to be unleashed upon him, turn him to cinders.

"Are you hurt?" said the light, which rocked back and forth, a silhouette coalescing around it as it emerged from the door. Marc breathed out a heavy sigh; it was a person with a high-powered electric torch. He grimaced as this light was shone in his eyes, and he held up a hand to fend it off. The illuminating beam turned to Jain in the wheelbarrow.

"Oh, she looks like she's in a bad way," said the person. It was an old lady in a dressing gown, gumboots on her feet. "Did you get caught in the flood?"

"Yeah," said Marc, not wanting to alarm the poor woman with the mad truth. "We're trying to get up to my parents' house."

"Which house?"

"It's the one with the green roof and the two rock walls."

"Oh, yeah, the walkers," said the woman, referring to Marc's parents' penchant for daily walks.

"That's the one."

"I'm Elsa, by the way," said the woman, offering a hand for Marc to shake, which he did. Her hand was dry, and the skin seemed fragile and thin.

"Marc," he said, "and this is Jain."

The woman nodded curtly, as if coming to a decision. "Let me help you. I'll get my car out of the garage."

"I'm sorry but we don't have anything to pay you with."

"Pay me? It's just a little lift."

Marc nearly burst into tears. Jain groaned feebly.

"Wait there," said Elsa.

In a few minutes' time Marc was loading Jain into the backseat, supervised by Elsa, who fretted around them.

"Are those burns?" she said, indicating not only Marc's feet but random patches of skin where embers and other burning materials had landed without him noticing.

"I suppose," said Marc, wishing she'd not pointed them out, because now they all hurt, a throbbing web of pain which seemed to encase his entire body.

"I saw the fires up on the ridge, bushfires I reckoned, but a weird thing to happen during a flood. Did you have to come through them?"

"Yes."

"You need an ambulance. You need to go to hospital."

"There's no way into town with this water everywhere," he said. He didn't have the heart to tell her the town had been swept into the sea, and that every hospital along this stretch of the coast would be burnt rubble under Godrisaur's monstrous feet by now.

Would she even believe him or understand?

The ground beneath them shook like a wobbling mass of jelly.

"What was that?" asked Elsa, looking around in stunned fear. "An earthquake as well? This is Australia. In all my years I've never—"

She was cut off by an echoing roar. It reverberated through the clouds overhead like the echoing voice of a vengeful God.

"What in the hell is that?" Elsa had to shout over the top of the sound, as it wasn't stopping. "That's some crazy thunder! Last thing we need is more rain."

Marc didn't have the heart to disabuse her of her comforting delusions. "Let's get Jain up to my parents' house so we can get out of your hair," he said when the sound finally paused. The old woman, looking more than a little shook, nodded and got in the driver's seat, the fear plain on her face.

She knows there's something more than a flood happening. But her imagination isn't as keen as mine and wouldn't conjure up the idea of a massive Kaiju, not yet, not until she's seen it with her own eyes.

"But I haven't seen it with my eyes either," he said under his breath as he got in the back with Jain. "Except when I close them, then the horrific monstrosity is right before me, bearing down on me, ready to destroy everything I hold dear."

I'm coming for you, said a voice in his head. It was thick and heavy, like lava running inexorably down the side of a volcano to envelop a town.

It was the voice of Godrisaur.

Another tremor rocked the earth as the Kaiju took another step, closing in on the final act of the story Marc saw playing out in his head.

I have to get Jain to safety, he said internally, and the selflessness of his intention was more powerful than any monster, drowning out that other voice and lifting him over this final hurdle.

***

My mind fills with a face. It is a human face, and in it I see a manifestation of the Anathema. I see a miniature version of my prey, though, unlike the Anathema, this being is presently weak and helpless. They do not really create this universe, this story, as they have convinced themselves is the case. They merely inhabit it, as do I. They are a character in a mythology, a monster out of time, given human form so that others believe their trickery. Now they have exposed themselves through their narcissism, made themselves into a focus of my hatred, an effigy of their whole race. They seek martyrdom. I can provide the death they crave.

The lodestone in my head reconfigures, turning towards this imago. They are my minor destiny, a fragment of the fate which will carry me a small step towards my final goal: a confrontation with the Anathema.

I realize now I am not strong enough to take on the sun alone. I need more power, and this power must come from will, the will of creation only a human mind possesses.

I am a monster. I can destroy but cannot create. I need the Yin to my Yang. I need to consume it, assimilate it into my being. Only when we unite can we spin in unison, encapsulate the world with our twin orbs of light and darkness.

***

Marc's parents' house was dark as Elsa revved her car up the steep driveway, spinning her wheels and leaving behind black tire marks on the yellow concrete.

Dad hates when people do that, thought Marc. *But what does any of that crap matter anymore?*

"I better get back home," she said as Marc helped Jain out the car. "That thunder is fit to burst a heck of a storm on us. Maybe it'll help with those bushfires though." She pointed out across the valley towards the city in the distance. "Looks like more fires up that way. This is the craziest damn weather I've ever seen. But what do you expect? This is Australia. Flood, then later the same year a bushfire, regular as the seasons. Right about figures we'd get a flood and bushfire at the same time eventually!"

Marc nodded, trying to focus on Jain, who was conscious and obviously in a lot of pain. He got his arms under her armpits and manhandled her across the driveway to a seat under the cover of the awning.

"You two will be alright?" Elsa asked, her worry plain, though whether it was for them or more for her own safety wasn't clear. She was already turning her car around, having spoken out the open window.

"Yeah, thanks so much. I don't know how I can repay you," he said, but the woman dismissed the notion with a wave and sped off down the driveway far too quickly, skidding the tires again.

Marc turned as he heard a familiar click, the bolt of the back door of the house being thrown. The door groaned like a floorboard in a haunted house as it was pushed open by a silhouette.

"What's all this?" said Marc's father Jacub, emerging with a lit candle in hand, wearing just a pair of ratty boxer shorts. He lifted the candle and peered out into the night, squinting to try to resolve their identities.

"Don't worry, it's me," said Marc.

"Marc? What are you doing here?"

"Jain's with me. She's hurt. We need help."

"Well, we can't get into town. There's a flood, if you haven't noticed."

"Trust me, I noticed."

"Hi, Dad," said Jain, her voice strained.

Jacub swung his candle around to illuminate Jain, sitting in a chair by the door. His eyes went wide when he saw her leg. "Bugger me dead, what's happened to you?"

"Exploding tree, if you can believe it," she said, managing a weak chuckle.

Marc started to explain. "We were trying to make it here to escape the tsunami that struck the coast and—"

Jacub held up a hand. "Hold up, tsunami? Like, a big wave?"

"Yes, if you'd let me—"

"Amelia!" Jacub called into the house. "Get out here. It's Jain and Marc. They reckon there's been a tsunami." He turned back to Marc. "So it's not a flood at all?"

"Not in the sense the valley normally floods due to rainfall, no," said Marc.

Jacub snapped his fingers. "I told your mum it hadn't been raining enough to flood."

Marc's mum Amelia came out wearing pajamas with a grumpy-looking cartoon cow on the front. Both she and the cow were holding cups of steaming coffee. She couldn't wake up without a brew.

"Coffee, Marc?" said Amelia, offering him the cup. "You can have this one, I'll make myself another."

"Actually, yeah, I could use something. I'm wrecked," he said, taking the cup gratefully.

"Jain's got a bad cut on her leg by the looks of it," said Jacub. "What about you, Marc, are you hurt?"

"I'll be right. Look after Jain for me, though, will you? I need to sit down."

"Come inside, the both of you."

"I'm alright here," said Jain.

A humungous roaring sound split the air, now familiar to Marc, but obviously a fresh shock to his parents, who both jumped. When it was done, Amelia asked, "What the devil is that?"

Devil indeed, thought Marc, gulping the black coffee down along with his fear.

"It's a monster," said Jain, and Marc was happy she was the one to say it. They'd have never believed him, claiming it was his overactive imagination.

But it is my imagination, isn't it? Yet somehow it has become real. I should never have written that book...

Marc's thoughts trailed away as a spike of pure panic rammed itself up his spine and into the base of his brain.

"Where's my laptop?" he shrieked in horror, looking around as if it might be on the ground by his feet.

"Your laptop?" asked his mother. "I don't know."

"I know you don't damned know!"

Marc's mind reeled as he tried to mentally trace back his steps. Everything that had happened felt like one long blur.

"Don't talk to your mother like that," said Jacub.

"Did you hear me? I said it's a monster," Jain piped up over the family bickering she was all too used to from them by now.

"You're just delirious from blood loss, darling," said Amelia.

The roar sounded again, louder this time, accompanied by the ground shaking.

It's coming this way, thought Marc, momentarily forgetting about his laptop, fear taking a hold of him. He knew the monster was after him now, that it saw something bright and shining in him, something for it to consume.

I gave it life, now it wants to assimilate me. I can give it the power to create. It wants to eat my imagination, use it against its enemy. I need a way out of this!

"I can write another ending," he said out loud, nearly frantic, and began searching for the laptop again, patting down his jacket as if it might be hiding in a pocket somehow.

"I'll get more candles and some water," said Amelia, seeming to ignore the quaking approach of Godrisaur, blotting it from her consciousness because it was too terrible to contemplate. "We need to look after that leg of yours, Jain."

This brought Marc's priorities back in line for a second and he looked at his girlfriend. Jain smiled at him, understanding his distress about the laptop, knowing him so well. But the smile was strained by pain, and this tugged at Marc's heart.

Once more the organ in his chest felt hot. It expanded and contracted painfully, seemingly far too big to be contained in his body as it thumped like a hammer striking a bell, tolling the death-knell of their collective doom.

No, we don't all have to die here. Godrisaur only wants me.

20

I'm coming for you. You have created me in your mind. I will live forever. As long as you think of me, it is so. Your imagination is my form. I know you see me in your thoughts. I am an infection, passing from one brain to the next, from one creator to another, each of them a little God which I will consume on my path to confront the Anathema.

There can be no death for me, no true death, for I am death itself, and I will be reborn in fire. The conflagration I have made here started with a tiny spark, a spark of an idea, and it will not be the end when it goes out, because ideas are infections of consciousness. They linger as long as they are passed from mind to mind, like one candle lighting another.

***

Amelia used her candle to light another one. She let it burn for a while, turning it so the flame melted the wax a bit. It flowed down the candle like blood onto a saucer. Amelia stood the candle in the pool of melted wax long enough for it to cool and hold it upright.

"Mum, I've got to go," said Marc.

"What? Go where?" She was rummaging through the cupboards.

"I need to lead the monster away. It's coming for me. I don't want you three, the people I care most about, to die as well."

"Don't be stupid, no one's dying. Here, take these bandages out to Jain. I think there's a propane camp stove in the garage. We can use that to boil some water."

"You're all set here, aren't you?" he asked. "For food and water, I mean."

"We've got weeks of food, and you've seen the store of water in the shed."

Marc smiled, recalling how, in better, simpler times, he'd helped refill the empty plastic bottles with water. For some reason they were all used cranberry juice bottles. One thing his parents certainly wouldn't be suffering from was scurvy or a urinary tract infection, the way they drank that stuff.

"And Jain," he said. "We can't get her to the hospital, but you'll clean and bandage her wound, right?"

"What do you think we're doing?" Amelia grabbed a fresh pack of soaps from the pantry, tore one free of the wrapping.

"She needs painkillers and antibiotics," said Marc.

"Oh, yeah, umm, okay… Well, we can use the painkillers for Dad's back, this packet here." She handed it to him. "And I have some antibiotics left over from that infected cyst. Yes, here we are. They're probably still good. They'll have to do. It's all we've got."

"Good, good," he said absently, his mind elsewhere now he knew Jain was getting some type of medical attention. He put the packets of tablets on the kitchen bench and gave her a big hug. "I love you, Mum. I hope I'll see you again one day."

He dashed out the door, leaving his mother stunned.

***

The cities are nothing but burning rubble behind me as I slosh through the waterlogged valley, rippling waves spreading out with each earthshattering footfall. But though I am mighty, I am not my own master anymore. I feel like a puppet on a string, a fish hooked on a line, a slave to the needle in my head, pointing the direction for me to take.

The Anathema has whispered a promise to me, dangling a tasty morsel before my fixed gaze. It is a bright soul, one that will catalyze my metamorphosis, take me to a new level.

I feel it become aware of my approach, and it moves to flee. Quickening my colossal stride, I close in for the kill.

***

"Stop him, Jacub!" called Amelia from inside the house.

"Bye, Dad, I love you," said Marc, giving Jacub a quick bear hug, but breaking free before the old man, still wiry strong, could grab him and hold him back. He need not have worried; his father was nearly deaf and didn't hear the shout, though he did frown in confusion.

Jain heard Amelia though, and also what Marc had said to his father. She perked up, even struggling up onto her good leg to hop after Marc as he went around the side of the house. Jacub followed after them, curious what Marc was doing, but more concerned with holding Jain up, who was very shaky and needed the support not to keel over.

"Where are you going?" asked Jain as Marc wheeled a pushbike out from behind the shed. "Look, if it's the laptop, forget about it. You'll write the story again, it's still in your head."

"Yes, it is in my head, and that's exactly why I have to go."

"Please, Marc, don't do this." She reached for him.

"Get your ass back inside," Jacub ordered Marc, his voice rising with his swift temper.

Marc looked at the pair of them as he mounted the bicycle. He desperately wanted to give Jain a kiss, but something told him there would be another chance, somehow, though maybe not in this life. He dared not go near her for fear Jacub would restrain him.

If I stay here they'll all die with me, and I can't bear to see that happen.

"I love you, Jain," he said instead. "Remember me."

Jain's moan was pitiful, the breaking of her heart audible in the cry as Marc pushed off and shot down the driveway on the bike.

21

"Fuck these fucking pedals," said Marc, panting hard from pain and exertion. The bottoms of his burnt feet were in agony and he was utterly exhausted, the coffee he'd drunk the only thing providing even the barest semblance of energy. He tried his best to ignore it all and continue, aware that every meter he covered was another between Godrisaur and his family. Luckily the street sloped downwards and he glided as much as he could, passing between groups of people who had come out of their homes, drawn by the noise. They were pointing off towards the horizon, their faces a mix of astonishment, fear, and confusion.

Marc didn't want to look at what they were pointing at, but he forced himself to. At first all he saw was the distant mountain ranges. They were a set of massive jagged silhouettes against a backdrop of a sky touched by the tiniest glimmer of dawn.

But one of the mountains was moving.

"Godrisaur…" Marc breathed, and the word seemed to carry on the wind to those around him, who repeated it in hushed awe as he passed.

As if in answer to its name, the moving mountain threw back its head like the top being blown off a volcano. A ray of brilliant light shot straight up into the sky, accompanied by a bestial roar to shake the heavens. This violent vibration was mirrored across the earth as the monster took another massive step. For a few terrifying seconds both the sky and ground were trembling so fiercely it almost threw Marc from his bike.

He fought hard to maintain his balance and reach the end of the street. There he was faced with a choice. He could head back the way they had come, retrieve the laptop—wherever it was he'd dropped it in his panicked flight—and try to create an ending which prevented disaster.

One look at the road leading uphill along the steep ridge and he dismissed this idea; he'd never physically make it. What's more, that way led closer to the monster, and he wanted to draw it away from the village and his family. So he turned towards the road which wound down into the valley.

***

I see you. You shine bright, little one. The souls in my guts sing with rapturous delight knowing you will soon join them in their agonizing abyss of blissful torture.

***

Marc was glad there were no cars on the winding, downhill road. He was moving fast and couldn't see well in the pre-dawn gloom. He surely would have flattened himself against the hood of any vehicle coming around the blind corners.

Though colliding with a car is just a slightly quicker way of committing suicide than my present course of action, he thought darkly.

Distracted, he swooped around another steep bend in the road, and this time he did hit something—a body of water.

Though not as disastrous as a head on with a car, it was still like colliding with a low wall, the bike brought to an abrupt halt beneath him, flinging him over the handlebars. He was thrown meters through the air and came down in a stinging impact, skidding over the surface of the water then tumbling beneath it. He came up gasping painfully, finding it difficult to get a breath in, the air knocked from his lungs by the impact.

"Fuck, fuck, fuck," he said, each word a sharp exhale followed by a too-shallow inhale. He felt lightheaded and was stunned by the crash. It took him a moment to register his surroundings. When he did he noticed the way the water around him trembled. He stood motionless and silent, watching as ripples expanded across it like the disturbed surface of a glass of water, registering the approach of something ponderously heavy.

***

I feel the warmth of the sun on my back, the true light of the Anathema shining its mocking rays upon me as it pokes its face above the horizon. But it doesn't matter anymore. I cannot chase it. It is too much for me. It will swoop overhead, mocking me with its brilliance and speed. I know I must grow, evolve into something to match its power.

I also notice there are more metal insects wafting on the breeze. Their jet engines hum like the fluttering of gossamer wings which vibrate too fast for the eye to see. They come with the new dawn to attempt once more to defeat me. But their weapons are no match for my primordial power. I shall shake my fist and clasp my claws and they shall join their brethren in fiery oblivion.

My prey is within reach. Nothing can stop me now, not even the Anathema.

***

Marc shat himself, the stinking brown effluent dispersing into the water as he tried to flee. He didn't notice or care. Every step he took was a struggle against the clinging embrace of the water as he waded through it, but he fought his way forward with all his remaining strength, propelled by an instinct for survival he was well aware would not be enough to save him.

Godrisaur was here, and Marc knew in his heart—which beat in unison with the monster's massive steps—that there was no escape.

22

Finally, I am here. You are here. We can be together, bonded forever in death.

Your death.

The wheel turns on the screw of creation and destruction, a moment of pure fate where our destinies align and become one. You shiver, stranded in a mass of water, looking up with wide eyes in which your destroyer—me—is reflected in miniature.

I open my mouth, swallowing the sun as I do, making way for you to pass down my gullet and join it inside me.

***

Marc would have fainted if he wasn't paralyzed with terror. His whole body shook, yet he was rooted to the spot, staring up at Godrisaur as it loomed over him. The monster was everything he'd seen in his visions. Then it had seemed small and distant, threatening yet somehow sanitized. Now it was viscerally real, so close and so large it blotted out the sky. It rose like an ancient monolith of stone, the rocky scales glowing demonically with internal fire. High among the clouds was the head, part lizard, part demon, a manifestation of every one of his nightmares. It stooped to inspect him with eyes which shone orange and yellow like the caldera of an erupting volcano.

So, this is how I die, thought Marc. *My end is a mystery no longer, as it has been my entire life, unknowable until this moment, yet now so clear—crushed or eaten by a horrible monster born of my own dreams, all alone in some field in the middle of nowhere.*

For a split second he regretted leaving Jain, and would have preferred to die by her side.

But not if it meant her dying as well, he thought, gaining some solace in the fact that he'd given her the best chance of survival he could. *I just pray I'm far enough away, that I've led it off on a different path.*

The monster was no longer roaring, just silently inspecting him, as if relishing his impending death. But Marc could hear a sound that resembled a roar. It was a rush of air, rising in pitch and culminating in a sonic boom.

The monster opened its mouth, a wide, dark chasm which led to a nightmare realm, and bent down. That awful head seemed to Marc to be moving in slow motion, or perhaps his senses were speeding up, his brain working frantically to take in every tiny piece of information in an attempt to find a way out of his predicament.

As the monster doubled over, the clear dawn sky became visible beyond. It was swarming with dark spots. For a moment he thought they were birds silhouetted against the light of the new day. This seemed fitting to him, a beautiful and poetic last sight before he passed.

The dark spots grew quickly, resolving into large black bombers with sharp, angular wings. Marc enjoyed the briefest moment of elation, his heart expanding in a surge of hope that they would kill the beast and he would be saved.

Godrisaur lunged down, mouth open wide. Everything went dark as the huge jaws closed and swallowed Marc in a single gulp.

***

I throw back my head in triumph, feeling the satisfying morsel slide down into my belly, its soul brighter than most. But I do not have time to enjoy my meal in peace; the human flies buzz around my head, swarming me in dense packs. I swat them away in annoyance, but these are swifter than their dead cousins, evading my blows as they shit on me in a disgusting rain which lands on my shoulders and back.

A massive explosion whites out my vision, another slams the doors of my ears, deafening me. A third and a fourth explosion crack away portions of my scaly hide, exposing magma flesh beneath. More bombs go off inside these gaping holes, tearing me apart from the inside with their atomic fury.

My body fights to regenerate, but it cannot do so fast enough to combat such horrific damage. My consciousness flees into the small sun hiding in my belly and cowers there as I am blown to pieces by nuclear bombs, my corporeal form erupting like a supervolcano. Rocky chunks of my flesh are thrown kilometers into the sky. My blood runs like a river of lava, quenched in the floodwaters of the valley, huge banks of hissing steam rising. I collapse like a shattered stone monument brought low by an earthquake, my hubris exposed to the world as my body disintegrates.

All that is left of me—the star at my core—rises up from the ruins of my former self. It floats up into the sky like the specter of a slain God, trailing a stream of gossamer sparkles. These shining dots are the souls which I captured. Now they must follow me into the next life, fueling my metamorphosis into a new monstrous form.

I will rise like a phoenix from the ashes of my fiery destruction, a brilliant new light to rival the Anathema. And though the dawn sun's red light washes the landscape with blood—my blood—it shall feel my wrath yet.

The Godrisaur you have known ever so briefly is dead, my destructive presence at an end for now, but in the chrysalis of the second sun, I shall be reborn!

Check out other great

Cryptid Novels!

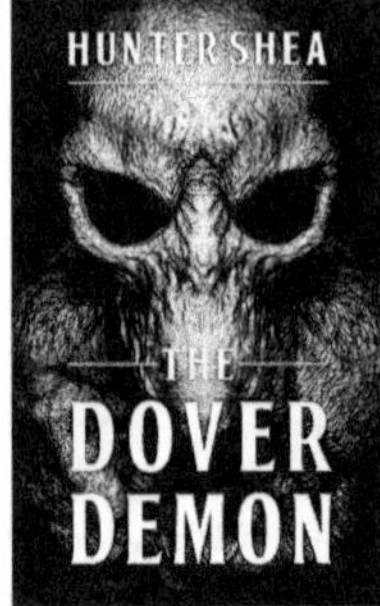

Hunter Shea

THE DOVER DEMON

The Dover Demon is real...and it has returned. In 1977, Sam Brogna and his friends came upon a terrifying, alien creature on a deserted country road. What they witnessed was so bizarre, so chilling, they swore their silence. But their lives were changed forever. Decades later, the town of Dover has been hit by a massive blizzard. Sam's son, Nicky, is drawn to search for the infamous cryptid, only to disappear into the bowels of a secret underground lair. The Dover Demon is far deadlier than anyone could have believed. And there are many of them. Can Sam and his reunited friends rescue Nicky and battle a race of creatures so powerful, so sinister, that history itself has been shaped by their secretive presence? "THE DOVER DEMON is Shea's most delightful and insidiously terrifying monster yet." – Shotgun Logic Reviews "An excellent horror novel and a strong standout in the UFO and cryptid subgenres." –Hellnotes "Non-stop action awaits those brave enough to dive into the small town of Dover, and if you're lucky, you won't see the Demon himself!" – The Scary Reviews PRAISE FOR SWAMP MONSTER MASSACRE "B-horror movie fans rejoice, Hunter Shea is here to bring you the ultimate tale of terror!" – Horror Novel Reviews "A nonstop thrill ride! I couldn't put this book down." – Cedar Hollow Horror Reviews

Armand Rosamilia

THE BEAST

The end of summer, 1986. With only a few days left until the new school year, twins Jeremy and Jack Schaffer are on very different paths. Jeremy is the geek, playing Dungeons & Dragons with friends Kathleen and Randy, while Jack is the jock, getting into trouble with his buddies. And then everything changes when neighbor Mister Higgins is killed by a wild animal in his yard. Was it a bear? There's something big lurking in the woods behind their New Jersey home.Will the police be able to solve the murder before more Middletown residents are ripped apart?

Ian Faulkner

CRYPTID

Be careful what you look for. You might just find it.1996. A group of 14 students walked into the trackless virgin forests of Graham Island, British Columbia for a three-day hike. They were never seen again. 2019. An American TV crew retrace those students' steps to attempt to solve a 23-year-old mystery.A disparate collection of characters arrives on the island. But all is not as it seems. Two of them carry dark secrets. Terrible knowledge that will mean death for some – but a fighting chance of survival for others. In the hidden depths of the forests – man is on the menu. Some mysteries should remain unsolved...

Eric S. Brown

LOCH NESS HORROR

The Order of the Eternal Light, a secret organization have foretold the end of the human race. In order to save all humanity, agents of the Order must locate the Loch Ness Monster and obtain a sample of its blood for within in it is the key to stopping the apocalypse but finding the monster will be no easy task.

www.ingramcontent.com/pod-product-compliance
Lightning Source LLC
Chambersburg PA
CBHW072238190626
46809CB00018B/2837

* 9 7 8 1 9 2 3 1 6 5 4 1 0 *